G000162378

She turned towards him, an apology for being found in his bedroom rising to her lips, but as her eyes met his she was mesmerised like a bird by a snake and a feeling of wild lust came over her again. She took a step towards him, the book still in her hand and as she did so he left the doorway and walked towards her. He seemed to hesitate as he reached her, but only for the very shortest moment. He lifted one hand and took hold of her chin, drawing her face towards his firmly, almost violently.

No, thought Amethyst to herself desperately. Not this soon – I mustn't. We ought to have a conversation first. Or something . . .

Today and Tomorrow

MANDY RICE-DAVIES

SPHERE BOOKS LIMITED

First published in Great Britain by
Fisher Publications 1986
Copyright © 1986 by Mandy Rice-Davies
Published by Sphere Books Ltd 1986
27 Wrights Lane, London W8 5TZ
Reprinted 1986

To my mother and father

TRADE
MARK

Set in Times

Printed and bound in Great Britain by
Cox & Wyman Ltd, Reading

PART ONE

AMETHYST

Chapter 1

For some reason Amethyst was suddenly reminded of her father, and the thought made her pause for a moment and smile. She wondered fleetingly whether he would have approved of his only child, but then, catching sight of her reflection in the full-length mirror on the opposite wall, she became absorbed once again in thoughts of the evening ahead. She still occasionally felt stage-fright before such dinner parties, though always in the end her innate grace and self-confidence stood her in good stead.

She felt warm and soft after her bath, and allowed herself to enjoy a few luxurious moments of self-congratulation and vanity before preparing herself for public approval. Amethyst had always wished to look like the tiny exquisite heroines of romantic fiction; she felt her name was too fanciful for strong dark eyebrows in a broad and humorous face. Her father had named her for the HMS *Amethyst* that had escaped the Chinese guns on the Yangtze and she was in a way thankful. Her name and her looks were about all she had as his legacy. Her height, her straight nose and Cherokee cheekbones were his, while her wide mouth was unmistakably her mother's. Such basic physical features were easy to trace to one parent or the other, but despite her knowledge of her father there was much in herself that still puzzled her. She found it hard to link her own determination and drive with either her dainty French mother or with the memory of her kind but somehow – even to a child – saddened father.

A knock at the door roused Amethyst from her introspection and she tried to shake the mood off. She had a hard-working evening ahead of her: she had to be charming and to appear charmed; she must be observant while not appearing to be taking too much in; she must stay alert and make mental notes on this powerful world in which she now moved and about which she was shortly to write. There was a knock on the door. After a perfunctory pause it opened. Amethyst turned and was irritated to see George Kelly simpering at her. She knew that he distrusted her and while she accepted that this was because of his almost fanatical loyalty to Brauner, she resented his exaggerated politeness and faintly super-cilious air. However, they kept up the appearances, as both knew that Brauner would never allow them to undermine each other to him. He would as soon drop them both as waste time with petty squabbles.

'Mr Brauner has just called to say that he is still in conference and is sorry that he is running late. He will meet you here in about an hour.'

The trouble with spending time with men of power, thought Amethyst, crossly, is that it became their prerogative, rather than the woman's, to be perpetually late.

'Thank you, George. Could you ask room service to send up some Krug?'

Amethyst never drank much as a rule, but now she felt she needed buoying up while she got on with dressing.

As the door closed behind George she turned to her dressing table and began carefully to make herself up. She knew the pureness of her skin and her English colouring were among her finest features, and made no attempt to compete with the Joan Collinses of smart American life. Time enough for that when she had lost the advantages of youth. However, she always enjoyed the mental as well as

4

the physical preparation that painting her face gave her for whatever lay ahead. While she was absorbed in this, room service brought her her champagne and she sipped at it pleasurably as she concentrated on her face. She felt an almost sensual pleasure as she outlined her mouth with a strong, dark pink, and subtly brought out the fine lines of her cheeks and chin. It always amused her how, no matter how ambitious and career-minded women became, the majority of them still worked hard at their appearance and thought obsessively about their wardrobes. It just showed how success and femininity could live easily together.

She turned to the bed where the dark purple dress of heavy silk was laid out for her, her underwear and stockings neatly folded beside it. Amethyst loved this dress – it was the favourite of her 'big hitters'. She knew Brauner loved her in it and was proud that it looked worth every cent of the nineteen hundred dollars she had spent on it. She rolled the silk of her stockings up her legs and toyed with the fancy of being an old-fashioned courtesan. The idea left her head almost as soon as it appeared: she knew how much more life meant to her than the highly agreeable extras of silk stockings and Bill Blass dresses. She pulled on her dress with a trace of tomboyish abruptness almost as a reaction to her fantasy, and then turned to her jewel box with its predictable over-emphasis on amethysts. She sometimes wished she had been called Sapphire which would at least have matched her eyes and would have taxed her lovers' ingenuity and wallets further. It was lucky no one knew she had been named after the escaped *Amethyst* or she might well have been subjected to endless bad jokes in glass bottles. As she stood, ready at last, tall, slim and undeniably striking with her shining blonde hair and dark brows conspiring to emphasise the deep blue of her wide-set eyes, she felt

5

happiness surge up within her. Everything had turned out so well. And all through Sylvia, really . . .

As if on cue the telephone rang. She picked up the receiver and heard her friend's shrill, forceful voice.

'Amethyst, darling, Sylvia here. I know Henry's terribly busy with the Israeli Prime Minister, and I am just really ringing to check everything is all right. It's all wonderful here. The flowers are perfect and chef's too sweet for words. He's organised the whole thing and it all fits perfectly so no one need worry about who's who or what's what . . .'

Amethyst smiled to herself as Sylvia rambled on. One thing that everyone *would* be minding about tonight was who was who and what was what. Sylvia was one of the most important supporters – socially and financially – of the Republican party, and her dinners were always triumphs of good organisation, tact, excellent food, wine and company. As Amethyst listened and murmured encouragement her mind went back to her first meeting with Henry Brauner, only six months before . . .

It had been in London, and Sylvia had been staying in the Dorchester for a fortnight to go to the theatre and catch up on old friends' gossip. Amethyst had met her a few months earlier in New York, where she had gone to follow up a story which had arisen when a well known socialite and her journalist companion were jailed for smuggling cocaine into England. While partying in a style that suited both her inclinations and her story, she had met Sylvia Benson, a super rich widow who spent a good deal of her husband's money on furthering the cause of the Republican party, both through massive donations and enormous political parties, dinners and balls. Matthew Benson had been a Southern States tobacco millionaire, and Sylvia, a sharp faced, attractive and warm-hearted

New York Jewess, had fallen for his languid Southern charm and easy generosity of both purse and spirit. He had died young, leaving Sylvia childless and genuinely bereaved. She had never remarried and never would, but her fidelity to her dead husband was completely unsentimental and only her very closest friends realised how often she still thought of him, and how much of what she did was still guided by her loyalty to him. Now, fifteen years later and in her late fifties – she had been fifty-nine for at least three years – her energy was directed towards various charities and political organisations and her warmth towards people from all stages of her life whom she regarded as her waifs. Amethyst was one of these. Sylvia had been immediately captivated by this attractive and obviously intelligent English journalist, and liked the transparent changes of mood she saw in the girl. While being as willing to enjoy a party as anyone, she seemed also to have a thoughtful and serious side to her nature, and even while in the middle of the most enjoyable party, there seemed to be a part of her that held back from the antics of those around her and observed them all, though without malice. Sylvia also felt a loneliness in Amethyst which she could understand, though she didn't know its cause.

Having met, the two women spent much of the remaining week of Amethyst's stay together, and despite the differences in age and circumstances struck up a true friendship. Amethyst had been one of the first people Sylvia had called when she arrived in London. Amethyst had been excited to hear from her; she had feared that Sylvia would be one of those ships that pass in a journalist's night. It had been two months, and yet it was as though they had left each other only the week before.

'Darling,' the voice had begun, without identifying itself – quite rightly, as there could be no doubt at all as to whom it belonged. It was a voice that some of the most powerful people in America were not ashamed to recognise and even to obey. 'I'm in London for a few weeks and of course we've got to meet. I want you to come to a party I'm throwing in the Dorchester on the twentieth. I have some people I must entertain and you must meet them. I presume you know of Henry Brauner? Well, of course you do – even the English must have woken up to him by now.'

Amethyst grinned. Sylvia spent a great deal of time being amazed at how totally apathetic most of the English were politically.

'Every high-school kid in America has more idea about what's going on than most of your so-called educated English gentlemen,' she would explode. Amethyst, however, though not really a political journalist and without taking any strong stance to right or left, kept herself well-informed and open-minded, and did of course know of Henry Brauner. Brauner was the white hope of the American Republican party and Amethyst had become aware in her brief acquaintance with Sylvia how completely involved she was with the party. Brauner's whole career had been aimed at the forthcoming elections. After step by well-considered step, he was now poised to move into the position he most wanted – the Secretary of State. While Sylvia's backing of the Republicans was whole-hearted and all-embracing, Brauner was her particular favourite, and it was he whom she was most interested in promoting. This party was to be one such promotion. She felt that every bit of publicity he could have – in 'apathetic' England as well as in America – could only be good.

'Well, it's really for Henry,' Sylvia continued, 'and you might find the whole thing interesting. Mind you, we don't want any "inside stories". Other people are going to deal with that side of things. I want you there as your own sweet self and without the word "Press" hanging over your head all evening – if you see what I mean. Now can you make it?'

'Try and stop me! What time does it start?'

'Six. I've got the Oliver Messel Suite with the roof terrace, so there'll be plenty of room. But first we've got to get you some clothes.' This was a point of disagreement. Amethyst had gone remarkably far in her career in a very short time. She had the knack, which some English girls possess, of being able to dress well on not much money, and although she now earned more than she would have dreamed possible three years earlier, she still felt guilty at over-extravagance in her wardrobe. She felt somehow that once she joined the band of exclusively dressed women that every capital city knows and loves to see, she would be out of her depth, and would soon go under. She also had a faintly feminist feeling (probably her only one) that if she were too expensive to look at, people would not take her seriously.

Sylvia's view was quite the opposite. She held firmly to the opinion that it was a woman's – and indeed a man's – duty to look as fine as possible all the time. And, she argued, if the talent was strong enough it would assert itself, no matter what superficial impression other people might gain from a girl's dress or the amount of shirt-cuff a man was showing.

Amethyst secretly longed to be won over completely to Sylvia's point of view – she loved to buy and to wear clothes that showed their class and reminded her of how successful she was becoming.

The other problem about shopping with Sylvia was her immense generosity which had to be curbed at every turn.

'I know what you're going to say,' Sylvia announced, 'but I have to get myself fitted out as well – I told you how I love shopping in London – and it's so much more fun with a companion. And, darling, these people are special. I want you to shine. I want us *all* to shine. Now let's meet early tomorrow and spend a glorious day.'

'The "glorious day" isn't all that we'll spend,' laughed Amethyst. 'But why not? I'd love a treat and I'm longing to see you.'

They did indeed have a wonderful day and Amethyst was successfully persuaded into buying more than just a new dress for Sylvia's party. After an exhausting time they joined up with two of Amethyst's friends – Dan Murray, with whom she was just beginning to feel comfortable again after the end of their affair, and a colleague of his, Jeremy Whittaker, a blue-eyed if ageing bachelor whose charm could always be relied upon. Amethyst found him good company, but had seen enough of him by the end of an evening. He was too conscious of his attraction and wit for Amethyst to feel wholly comfortable with him. Sylvia insisted on 'taking in a show', an expression at which even Amethyst winced inwardly, but Amethyst felt that her friend had enjoyed their day and evening, even though Whittaker became a little drunk and rather less charming, without seeming to notice.

Sylvia's party was several days later, and Amethyst arrived looking her best in a new dress of shimmering blue-green. She felt a little nervous, but was amused to see Whittaker across the room, looking sheepish, though every other inch the working journalist. She glanced around and seeing no one else she immediately recognised, thought she would cross the room towards him and see what happened.

She had only taken two steps when Sylvia was at her side, covered in rubies and looking perfect in a red Valentino dress that accentuated her extremely slim figure. She kissed Amethyst warmly, leaving an outline of geranium red lipstick on her cheek. Amethyst was immediately introduced to a pleasant-looking young man, Isaac Meyer, who was one of the public relations men attached to Brauner.

From then on, Amethyst relaxed and began to enjoy the party. Everything fitted. The view out over Hyde Park was at its best, with the early evening sun filtering through the few clouds and warming the faces and backs of those who stood by the window or out on the roof garden. It was Amethyst's favourite time of year, near enough to summer for everyone to revive and begin to dream again of long hot days and drinks on the terrace, but not far enough into the season for disillusion to set in along with another rainy English summer. Amethyst always reacted strongly to the changes in weather, becoming euphoric every year for the first few days of sunshine.

Tonight, despite her initial unease, she knew how good she looked and she always enjoyed talking to other people from whom she could learn and against whom she could test her wit and opinions. She was in an argumentative mood this evening, and felt like a 'real' conversation, rather than the endless small talk that is sometimes a trap at such parties. She was at her most mercurial and her most charming when in this mood. Even her best friends were often unsure whether she was arguing for something about which she cared passionately, if she was arguing simply to irritate someone she found pompous or dull, or if she was enjoying some complicated private joke only she could understand. She would swing unpredictably from an expression of suppressed fury to a broad grin or an unrestrained laugh. And all in a matter of moments.

She was preparing for battle with a perfectly straight-forward looking man who was very important 'in the City' who had just told her that he felt his politics were 'quite definitely to the right of Reagan's' (Amethyst would, in

11

normal circumstances, have declared herself a firmly dedicated Communist, but felt some loyalty was owed to Sylvia) when she saw Brauner across the room.

She stopped in mid breath. She had known from photographs that he was good looking, but had not realised quite how *distinguished* looking he was. It was not just his features – his thick grey hair, his brilliantly blue eyes with the disconcertingly small pupils (the journalist in her wondered fleetingly whether there could be a drug story here, but everything else in him gave the lie to that idea), the large aquiline nose, the well-defined firm mouth. Nor was it his dress, which was faultless in its understated and perfect elegance.

There was something else which made this not particularly tall man stand apart from the smiling and by now totally relaxed crowd which filled the room. Amethyst's concentration left the right-wing city potentate completely and as she smiled and chatted banally to him in the manner which she was sure he had expected of her, she covertly watched Brauner and the group he was with. She noticed that like her he did not seem to drink much, only occasionally taking a sip at what looked like whisky and soda. While he was joining in the conversation, smiling in an urbane way and appearing to enjoy himself, there was a quality of stillness about him which fascinated her. She sensed that he was totally alert and probably missed nothing.

With this thought she became abruptly conscious of herself and to her annoyance she began to blush. She turned back to her tycoon and speedily, but with her usual charm, wound up the conversation and excused herself so that she could go and find Sylvia. *Why* had Sylvia not introduced her to Brauner as she had repeatedly promised? Although Amethyst had until then been enjoying the party and had only vaguely wondered whether she would in fact meet its inspiration, she now felt that she could not leave until she had been introduced.

Sylvia, as it happened, found her first. 'Amethyst,' she shrilled. On the terrace a few pigeons scrambled for the skies. 'I've been looking all over for you. I meant to ask you when you came in, but it quite slipped my mind. Join us for dinner – I've booked a table downstairs at the Terrace, Anton knows we're coming and I've left the menu to him. He won't let me down. You haven't made any other plans, have you? Do come. Have you met Henry yet?' Amethyst shook her head and tried to look just as interested as she ought to be, but not as interested as she really felt.

'Well?'

Amethyst nodded, irritated at her sudden inability to speak, and then gabbled, 'Sylvia, I'd love to, and yes – no – I haven't met Henry Brauner yet and would love to.' All in one breath. Sylvia looked surprised.

'Good, great, we'll be going down in about half an hour,' she said, and rushed off to speak to another guest.

The following half hour passed soon enough. Amethyst was pleased to see one of her closest friends, Suzy Porter, whom she had met during her first weeks in London. Suzy had then been an aspiring journalist, but had soon given up and was now working successfully for a PR firm – the one hired to cover Brauner's stay in England.

'Suzy! What a surprise. I had no idea you'd be here. What have you been doing? I haven't seen you for ages!'

'Oh, the same old thing. I was lucky to get in on Brauner. The boss had to pull out at the last minute. Are you joining the dinner party?'

Amethyst nodded. 'And you?'

'Yes, although I wasn't expecting to. I don't think many people have been invited. Have you met the hero of the hour?'

'Not yet.' Amethyst was feeling less desperate about it now she had the dinner to look forward to, and the hope that she would be near enough to him for conversation. While talking to Suzy, Amethyst had been frantically trying to think who else would be going to dinner and working out the probable *place-à-table*. She had a feeling that there was little chance of her sitting next to him.

Just then Sylvia caught her eye and Amethyst moved towards the doorway. Brauner arrived beside Sylvia at the same moment and Amethyst had to force herself to keep calm as she was at last introduced to the man who, for some reason, held such a fascination for her. She looked up at his face and was immediately struck by the intensity of his eyes, made bluer by his deep, healthy tan. He looked like a man familiar with power and she sensed – or thought she sensed – a compressed violence in him that frightened her. As Amethyst stood there locked in his shock-blue stare she was suddenly filled with a wild unfamiliar longing. She wanted to be dragged away by him and made love to completely and immediately. Amethyst was feeling something she had so far never felt for a man – an overwhelming physical attraction that chopped her off at the knees. Christ, this is it, she thought, lust at first sight. She felt giddy and damp all over. Dan, her first lover, had always been gentle and loving towards her in and out of bed and he had set the standards by which she had measured her sexual relationships. Amethyst had in the main been as moderate in sex as she was in her other pleasures (she had even congratulated herself on this) so how could she, with the contempt she had always felt for casual sex, long to be pinned down in a bed and be wildly made love to by this stray American? The thought of it left her deeply shaken and at the same time intensely excited.

'Now who hasn't met who?' Sylvia, who had been

caught in the ripples of this electric biochemistry, suddenly found her voice and as usual it rose above the others and took command. 'Henry, this is Amethyst Barclay. Amethyst, I didn't know you knew Suzy, and Isaac I've introduced you to. The Jays are just ahead of us, I'll introduce you when we get to the Terrace.

'Now let's go down, we're running late and we must keep Anton happy.'

In no time at all the introductions were over and the party was on its way downstairs. Suzy came up close to Amethyst.

'Are you all right? she whispered anxiously. 'You look a bit shaky.'

'I am.' Amethyst tried to laugh, but it came out weakly. 'Don't worry, I'll be all right in a second.' Amethyst was disturbed that Suzy had noticed anything. If Suzy had, perhaps it had been all too obvious to Brauner.

She had pulled herself together by the time they reached their table and was immediately disappointed at being put in a place where there was no chance at all of talking to Brauner. She was sitting next to Harold Jay, an American property dealer. Amethyst had heard of Jay, one of Brauner's oldest friends and strongest supporters. She thought she had been told that Jay had poured a lot of money into fostering Brauner's political career, and that he still financed much of Brauner's political campaign. Jay was quite a lot older than Brauner, and was a loud, domineering man. Very much the motivated American, Amethyst thought, and playing the role up to the hilt. Although he was genial and polite, Amethyst didn't really take to him. He was smart, but seemed to do his best to disguise it, and Amethyst found this unnerving. On her right was Isaac Meyer, the PR man to whom she had been introduced earlier on. The only other people she had not met before were Kelly, Brauner's personal assistant, who

15

didn't seem to be a very interesting or positive looking man, and Mary Jay who was pretty in an uninspiring way and seemed much younger than her husband.

I bet she was his secretary and he bullies her unmercifully, thought Amethyst, watching how Jay addressed her with a politeness so perfect it was almost insulting.

Brauner was sitting diagonally across from Amethyst, but too far away for any real chance to talk. Occasionally she met his eyes, though she tried hard not to. She felt ridiculous – like a teenager – but to her friends she looked more attractive than they had ever seen her. Both Sylvia and Suzy, who knew her well, noticed and admired her poise and charm this evening. Tonight she looked beautiful. Although Sylvia and Jay did most of the talking, it was undeniably Amethyst who held the attention of everyone at the table. Meyer, sitting beside her, felt a wild hope that her charm and wit were directed towards him and was hopelessly smitten.

'So you're a journalist, Miss Barclay. Are you covering the campaign?'

Meyer's diffident smile was appealing but Amethyst barely noticed it.

'No – and please call me Amethyst. I'm a friend of Sylvia's which is why I'm here. Of course I'm sure I'll write about the campaign at some stage.'

'You have a very beautiful name.' Meyer lost interest in the career conversation and set out to pay court to her.

'My father was in the Navy.' She waited to see if the penny dropped. It didn't.

Meyer felt desperate, knowing he was losing her attention. His hand clenched around his wine glass and he tried to think of something interesting to say. Suddenly the glass shattered between his fingers. Amethyst turned to him, startled.

'He did that on purpose,' she realised, and felt sorry for him.

Meyer was ashamed of his impulse to show off, although everyone treated it as an accident and with the minimum of fuss.

Brauner drank little and said less. He was aware, with that uncanny ability that some men possess, that he was having an effect on Amethyst. It was not an arrogant or egotistical knowledge, rather it was instinctive. Women interested Brauner – their bodies, of course, but more than that. He was intrigued by the way they thought, the way they reacted . . . especially to him. He liked to possess women physically – which man does not? – but every seduction was also an intellectual challenge. He had to feel that when he made love to a woman she was dominated . . . not physically, necessarily, because love-making took many forms, but intellectually. He liked clever, witty, intense women; he liked to be challenged, tested even, but in the end he had to be the winner. He had realised with a kind of cold calculation that his attraction was a combination of looks, physique, and power but with an extra ingredient, intellectual maleness, as well. He found himself thinking that Amethyst was worthy of him, that she had established something to him, and he to her, that the male and the female had looked at one another, reached an understanding, and all that remained was time. Now he revelled in the sensual. He could feel the wave of desire and sexuality flowing from her to him, and that never failed to stimulate both his desire and his own sexual responses. He luxuriated in that, as a man will luxuriate in champagne or a fine cigar. One day soon, he realised with a rush of blood, he would possess her. It was a man's feeling, as old as time, as primeval and natural as hunger.

The conversation was general, with the minimum of

political talk. Amethyst watched Jay as he stabbed his steak viciously and admired the blood that oozed out.

'Not many good steaks this side of the Atlantic,' he announced, 'but this is OK.'

'You think it's bad in Europe, you should try it in the Bahamas. I have a house in Nassau which is wonderful in every way except for the meat. When I get back I just head for the nearest cow and chew. Like they say in Texas – cut off its horns, wipe its ass, and put it on my plate.' Sylvia had the gift of looking surprised when she said something vulgar which always raised a laugh.

'Do you go out there often?'

'The Bahamas? Two or three times a year, sometimes more. It depends. Perhaps we could all go out there for a holiday after the elections!'

Jay smiled and half-nodded in acknowledgement. 'That would be swell. But before that, how about Florida? I have a house in the Keys – Henry knows it well.'

'Harold lends it to me sometimes,' Brauner explained. 'If he ever offers you the loan, Amethyst, I should take it up. It's one of the most private places I know.'

'When we're there, we live in the main house, but Henry prefers the cottage.' Mary Jay had a quiet, pleasant voice, and sounded as though she was not really expecting anyone to listen to her.

'Cottage is a modest word for real comfort,' Brauner told Amethyst. 'Mary's cook is excellent. You feel completely secluded, the sea is as warm as anywhere I've swum . . . Harold, I think I'm talking myself into inviting myself down for a weekend when we get back home.'

Everyone enjoyed dinner. Even Mary Jay became forthcoming under the influence of a little drink and Brauner's friendly gallantry. Amethyst warmed towards Jay, although still basically distrusting him. The food was delicious. Anton had excelled himself. Sylvia, nibbling at

18

the *fraises de bois* soufflé, was on her favourite subject –
the political apathy of the English – when Amethyst,
feeling flippant and wanting to change the subject,
remarked: 'You in America are so politically aware at the
age of ten that by the time you are twenty you're either
closet fascists or closet communists.'

It was one of those thoughtless comments that fall into a
pool of silence and therefore become much worse. Suzy,
who knew how her friend was prone to say this sort of
thing and could be as bad or worse herself, looked at her
sympathetically. Sylvia looked slightly hurt, Brauner and
Meyer surprised, Jay cross and Mary nervous. Even the
soufflé seemed to collapse.

It was Kelly who broke the silence. 'I don't expect that
you mean that we are all fascists,' he said, stiffly, 'and
closet communists are rather the British forté.'

'My dear Mr Kelly, in Britain *everything* is in the closet;
our politics, our sexual preferences, but above all our
brooms. The difference between our two countries is that
you take far too many things out of the closet that would
be better-off remaining in it.' Brauner laughed, an event
in itself. 'And I wouldn't say for one moment that all
Americans are fascists, that would be a disgraceful slur on
your great nation. Simply that rather too many generals
and politicians . . .' she caught Brauner's eye ' . . . act
like fascists when they feel their domestic or international
interests are threatened. But I don't expect to see the
swastika stamped on the Stars and Stripes.'

Brauner applauded lightly. 'Touché, Miss Barclay,
America considers itself duly chastised.'

Amethyst was confused. She felt she had been witty,
but knew that she had been upstaged, put in her place
somewhat. She resolved to be more careful after that.
Amethyst was irritated at herself. She looked over
towards Brauner a few times, but he was engrossed in

19

Sylvia and Mary Jay and did not return her glances. Although he seemed to be perfectly at ease and enjoying himself, she noticed with a trained journalist's eye that he constantly fidgeted with his wine glass or with small pieces of bread on the table. It was as though the stillness in him – one of the qualities she had first noticed – allowed him this one small nervous outlet. His hands were very long and fine, in contrast with his body, which was broad-shouldered and well built. Amethyst became absorbed in watching his beautiful and well-kept fingers crumbling his bread, until she became aware that there was something distinctly odd about the right hand. She concentrated on it for a few seconds and then Brauner leaned forward to light a cigarette for Mary Jay, and she realised that he could not bend the little finger at all and that its tip was missing. It fascinated her but, suddenly self-conscious, she turned back to Jay.

The party broke up not long after. Brauner and Amethyst had barely exchanged a word. The strength of the first wave of desire had left her, but Amethyst still felt helplessly drawn towards this man and disappointed that they had not been thrown together more satisfactorily.

As she was kissing Sylvia goodbye and thanking her, Brauner came up behind her and touched her arm lightly. 'How are you going home?' he asked blandly. The look and the touch so weakened her defences that she could barely answer that she had her car.

'I'll walk you to it,' he said and Amethyst nodded. They walked in silence until they reached her white Porsche Targa. She felt a childish satisfaction that her car was as smart as her company, and hoped Brauner would notice it.

Then Brauner spoke. 'I'm leaving London Wednesday and would love to see you before then. How about a drink here tomorrow? I'm in Suite 506. I'll be in a conference until about seven – we could meet then.' He was telling her almost more than asking her. Amethyst nodded again, glad that it was dark because she felt herself blushing.

'I'll see you tomorrow, then. Thank you. Goodnight.' He watched her drive away before he turned and walked back to the hotel.

The next evening Amethyst was stupidly excited. She had talked to Suzy and they had had a long post-mortem on the drinks and dinner party, but for some reason Amethyst had told her friend nothing of her attraction to Brauner, partly because there was nothing to tell and partly because she did not really want Suzy to know that she was meeting him again that night.

'What were you up to, walking out with a stranger?' Suzy teased. 'Did you go night-clubbing?'

'No, he just walked me to my car.'

'And then what?'

'Nothing.'

'Don't be silly, Amethyst. He's the best-looking thing I've seen for years, you *can't* just go walking out with him and do *nothing*. Did you make a date? What did he say?'

'Nothing, really, Suzy.'

'Stop saying "nothing". I can't believe you didn't take him in. Did you see those eyes? What a man. Didn't you fancy him at all?'

'I hardly talked to him.' Amethyst evaded the question, but not very successfully.

'That means yes,' Suzy triumphed. 'Oh well, if you don't want to tell me . . .' She paused suggestively.

This was meant to lead Amethyst on, but she stayed silent. Now she wished she had told her friend about the date, if only for moral support on the question of what to wear. She had returned to her flat far too early and was feeling over-eager and excited so had spent a lot of time pacing the floor before frantically tidying the already pin-neat flat. Even more than her expensive clothes and car her home symbolised her success and the security it brought. Even if her work was suddenly to become unfashionable, she would still have her flat with its light, airy rooms to comfort and protect her.

It was a one-bedroomed apartment in Maida Vale; the sitting room had to be used for her to work in as well as for entertaining her friends, so it was as functional as it was decorative. The walls were a coral pink, a colour Amethyst knew was flattering to blondes. Her skin reflected its warm glow, and the room always looked cosy in winter and cool in summer. Thick Persian rugs neatly covered the stripped pine floorboards, and bunches of white flowers were all over the room. One huge olive-wood table was used both for dinner parties and, more often, for Amethyst to strew her work over. There was a large sofa and two old-fashioned and very comfortable wing chairs. The room looked very lived-in, a mixture of old furniture from home and things she had picked up over the last few years.

Amethyst pinched a few dead flowers from among the bouquets and then went around the flat with a duster and a can of polish, relentlessly buffing every piece of furniture and twitching the few pictures straight. She revelled in the mixed smells of the flowers and the spray polish, wishing she had the time to get down on her hands and knees to wax the floor inch by inch as her mother had done every week at home. That was even more satisfying in both look and smell.

Finally she decided that she could allow herself to have a bath and change. Having spent all day fidgeting with nothing to pass the time until it was time to change, she now began to put it off. In spite of her energetic cleaning campaign, she began to feel edgy again.

'Stop it,' she said out loud with mock firmness. 'For a woman of twenty-eight, you're behaving like a star-struck teenager, Amethyst Barclay, and it won't do.'

She did a few more useless jobs, going into the kitchen to throw out some food left over in the fridge. Then suddenly she realised she was going to be late. In a panic, she rushed into the bathroom and turned the taps on full.

Afterwards she stepped out of the bath smelling deliciously of Floris Rose Geranium, and wrapped herself in a huge, soft, pale yellow towel. She loved the colour, but knew that as a blonde she could not wear it and so had to confine herself to secret splurges. She crossed to her bedroom and opened the cupboard which was inset along one wall of the room. She wanted to look demure tonight. She was sure Brauner must have sensed her strong attraction for him and did not want to meet him looking as though she were bent on seduction. She had almost made up her mind what to wear before her bath, but now she was indecisive again. She tried on three dresses in a row and rejected them all. The first was too close in colour to the one she had worn the night before, the second made her look like a Girl Guide on an outing (she had always liked it before) and the third showed far too much nipple.

Finally, she settled on a simple blue dress, low waisted and high at the front but with a very low back. Amethyst was proud of her back, and with good reason. Her only worry was that her skin, although soft and unblemished, had too much winter whiteness about it, but when she slipped the dress over her head and turned her back to the mirror she saw that its creamy whiteness contrasted well with the deep blue. She put on pearl earrings and decided that the whole effect was perfectly restrained. Finally she was ready to go.

Amethyst was a careful ten minutes late at the

Dorchester, and was shown up to Brauner's suite by an attentive bell-boy. However she was surprised to find no Brauner. Instead his PA, Kelly, was lying in wait for her.

'Miss Barclay.' He greeted her politely but without warmth. 'Mr Brauner has been held up and sends his apologies. He has ordered some champagne for you while you wait,' he gestured towards the low table by the sofa where two glasses stood by a bottle in its ice bucket. 'If you would care for anything else, it will of course be brought up.'

Amethyst was taken aback. She was not sure whether Brauner had ordered Kelly to entertain her along with the Krug while she waited, but before she had searched her mind for small talk Kelly solved her problem by excusing himself, leaving her alone in the room.

Amethyst poured herself a glass of the champagne and sat on the sofa. She picked up the *Spectator* which had been left on the coffee table and began to read Ferdinand Mount's article, but her concentration was fragmented. After a few minutes she began to feel as though she were waiting for a bus. She had looked at her watch six times and it was still only twenty-five to eight. She got up and began to walk around the room, amazed at how totally impersonal it was, although she knew Brauner must have spent at least a week there. It took Amethyst less than a night to make any room, whether in the Danieli or a bed and breakfast in Devon, totally her own. Her tidiness did not desert her, but her habits of carrying too many books and buying more wherever she went, and of cutting odd scraps out of newspapers and magazines, as well as the endless feminine paraphernalia and the pairs of shoes scattered under the bed or wherever she took them off (she had to admit to being untidy with shoes), meant she stamped herself on any room, regardless of austerity or comfort.

Having exhausted the possibilities of the sitting room, she wondered fleetingly about the bathroom and paused. Well, she could say she had needed to 'powder her nose' – or let it be assumed. And bathrooms were always a good means of judging someone's character. She opened a door and checked momentarily when she saw it led into the bedroom. However she could see the bathroom across the room and this decided her.

The bathroom was, disappointingly, as free from any hint of a personality as the sitting room had been. Completely ordinary toothpaste, a toothbrush (blue), shaving kit (not electric – that was something) and a cologne. It could all belong to almost any man. Only the cologne was expensive, but it was not that special.

Amethyst left the bathroom and crossing the bedroom saw a book by the bed and decided that having snooped so far it was too late to be coy. She bent to pick it up: *Don Quixote*. She smiled to herself. Even that did not give much away. She straightened, suddenly aware that someone was standing in the doorway behind her and sure it would be Brauner. She turned towards him, an apology for being found in his bedroom rising to her lips, but as her eyes met his she was mesmerised like a bird by a snake and a feeling of wild lust came over her again. She took a step towards him, the book still in her hand and as she did so he left the doorway and walked towards her. He seemed to hesitate as he reached her, but only for the very shortest moment. He lifted one hand and took hold of her chin, drawing her face towards his firmly, almost violently.

No, thought Amethyst to herself desperately. Not this soon – I mustn't. We ought to have a conversation first. Or something.

But despite herself she returned his kisses. She was dimly aware of him removing the book from her hand and dropping it to the floor. The next thing his cheek was against hers, his hands hard on her shoulders and his breath soft and warm in her ear. Her last effort at self restraint vanished as she felt him pull at the shoulders of her dress. It slipped down over her without effort.

'How can he have got the measure of this dress so quickly?' she wondered vaguely. 'And I thought I was looking *demure*,' quickly followed by, 'My God, his hands! How could a man have such hands?'

Tender and skilful, his hands were following the dress's progress to the floor, tracing the length of her spine, finding the two dimples at the base of her back and pausing there for a moment before reaching for her buttocks, holding their soft fullness and pulling her towards him.

The feel of his suit against her near-nakedness aroused her almost to desperation and once again she felt the urge for violence which she had so unusually experienced the night before. He put her from him for one second as with speed but an almost chilling calmness he took off his clothes. Amethyst swayed, too stupefied by desire to do anything other than marvel at the sight of his firm, expectant body. He pushed her back on the bed with one hand and with the other eased off her lacy knickers. Naked, she lay outspread, her arms at her sides, accepting his hands and his fingers, once again astounded at their practised skill and the primal power they had over her. Then as he brought his face down to suck her nipple, he plunged a finger deep inside her and, searching, found that magic spot which he stroked and caressed until her whole body was pulsating with sheer insanity. Now Amethyst was really panic-stricken – how did he know just how to touch and *where* to touch her? It was unreal, like being possessed by a spirit. She tried to move away from him but suddenly he was fierce;

his lips and teeth and tongue were everywhere, on her nipples, her breasts, her neck, her thighs and at last, when Amethyst was roused beyond containment, he forcibly drew up her legs behind his neck. Then pulling her towards him with his hands firm on either buttock he entered her hotly and forcefully, bringing her to the longest sweetest orgasm she had ever experienced. They still had not said a word.

Amethyst returned to her flat early the next morning, even more shaken than she had been when she left it the evening before, and with feelings as mixed. She had never been so thoroughly and expertly made love to, but the very fact that it had been with a stranger and one that she was quite likely never to see again disturbed her. She was sure that Brauner had to some degree felt as she had, but then to a man who had stepped out with so many of the world's beauties and was so obviously experienced, the night had in all likelihood been one of many and of no import. She had probably been just another pretty fuck; a way to release the energy that had been pent up by long hours of talk and negotiation.

Amethyst's wish to see him again was motivated almost entirely by lust, but there was also a fascination over and above that which the intimacies of the night before had not dispelled. She lay in her bath, the door ajar in case the telephone should ring, and as she soaped her long limbs she felt a thrill come over her; the marks which Brauner's hands and teeth had left on her flesh were all too apparent. One thing she could do, she decided, was to ring up the *Observer* and see if they wanted a profile done on him. Of course she would not mention the night before and her bruises need not come into it, but she could say she had met him at Sylvia's party and would write an article that would show him she was not just another blonde popsy to be loved and left.

The telephone did not ring and no flowers arrived. Amethyst knew that Brauner's aeroplane left around mid-morning, so by lunch time she had given up hope. She left the flat feeling dispirited and cross with herself for minding. She determined to concentrate fully on her work.

For the next few weeks she more or less succeeded, although the memory of Brauner's insistent hands would return to her at odd moments.

Her *Observer* idea was accepted.

'I like the way you see Brauner as such a *violent* man,' the features editor told her. 'It's a new approach.'

Amethyst smiled sweetly. Brauner would know what she meant.

Six weeks later Amethyst was sent to New York to interview Tina Brown, one of the successful English women journalists of her day. Amethyst was looking forward to meeting this paragon. Although keen on the assignment, she had another reason for going to New York – she wanted at least a chance of seeing Brauner again. She had not heard from him once since the night at the Dorchester. She had rung his Washington office and talked to a PR representative to check on a couple of biographical details for the article; making sure to leave her name and telephone number 'in case you would like anything added', but there had been no call. When the *Observer* article had appeared, she had again half-expected some sort of comeback – but nothing.

She had barely checked into her room at the Algonquin before she was on the telephone to Sylvia.

'Hello, Sylvia, I'm in New York for a few days – let's have lunch tomorrow.'

Amethyst knew she would have done the same had

there been no Brauner, but her ulterior motive made her voice sound weak in her own ears. Sylvia did not seem to notice anything and greeted her excitedly. Before long Amethyst had succeeded in bringing the conversation around to Sylvia's party.

'I'm so glad you enjoyed it, darling. I think it was a success. Even Mary Jay seemed to come out of herself a little at dinner. Of course Henry can charm anything if he bothers to try – that's the politician in him. Or perhaps it's the reason why he's such a good politician.'

'Chicken and egg?' suggested Amethyst.

'What? Oh yes, I suppose so,' answered Sylvia dismissively. 'Did you talk to him at all?'

'Who?' Amethyst said ingenuously. 'Oh, Henry. Well, not really at dinner' (or after, she thought) 'but he invited me for a drink the next day.'

'And did you go? Well of course you did. A journalist wouldn't miss such a chance. I saw your article on him, and wondered when you'd interviewed him.'

'I didn't interview him.' Amethyst wondered if she was going to get the giggles. 'We just – chatted. But it gave me the idea. I must go now, Sylvia. I'll see you at Le Relais at one tomorrow.'

'Now, please,' she thought as she hung up and sat with fists clenched on the edge of her bed, 'please let her mention to him that I'm in town. She must.'

It was not until the next afternoon, after she had lunched with Sylvia and talked as little as possible about Brauner, that she was given the message that Henry Brauner had rung. The receptionist looked at Amethyst curiously, wondering if it were *the* Henry Brauner who had rung this pretty English girl. Amethyst reached her room and was just deciding whether to ring him back immediately or wait for him to ring her again and risk his not doing so, when the telephone rang. She let it ring for a short time before she picked it up.

'Henry Brauner speaking. How are you fixed for dinner tonight?'

How her life had changed in those six short months, Amethyst thought, as she adjusted a bracelet on her now golden brown arm and checked that her earrings were in properly. She was now living what the *Daily Mirror* would call a 'champagne lifestyle', and loving every minute of it.

After the interview with Tina Brown, Amethyst had gone back to England to close down her flat and make arrangements for her new life. She decided to work on a series of stories about Brauner and the Republican campaign. His popular appeal was enough that public interest in him wouldn't wane whatever the outcome of the elections. Amethyst's reputation was sufficient for her to find a syndicate prepared to give her a good advance and generous expenses to follow the campaign and file weekly reports. Brauner had promised his full co-operation, which had been a great help.

When Amethyst had come back to New York a month later, it was with Brauner's official approval, but unofficially most people knew that she and Brauner were having an 'Affair'.

At the moment they were staying in Brauner's two connecting suites in the Regency Hotel on Park Avenue. Amethyst had everything she wanted, but she clung to as much of her independence as circumstances would allow and still worked hard at freelance writing for both English and American newspapers. Of course, she did not pretend that she could afford to live in quite this style on her money alone, and she knew that the expenses given her by her publisher for her work as biographer would not normally run to living in Brauner's suite. But she had to accept something from him if she wanted to be with him.

And she did. The sexual force which had first attracted them to each other, and which had consumed them both so totally in their first few months together, was still there. Their intimacy was complete and Amethyst was utterly happy in the relationship. She knew that Brauner's feelings for her must be deeper than he would admit. He had of course had many love affairs before her, but never one for so long and conducted so openly. Seeing Amethyst on Brauner's arm at a party was gossip column fodder in celebrity-conscious America: their combined good looks meant that they were often photographed together, and their alliance was common knowledge and accepted as such.

But there was a dark, puzzling side to Brauner. Without warning he would sink into a deep silent pit of depression, then as suddenly, he would spring back and resume his character like a man exchanging roles in a theatrical performance. He suffered nightmares from which he woke up screaming. When that happened Amethyst would switch on the light and take him in her arms, soothing him like a mother, but as soon as he regained possession of himself, he would push her away roughly, saying: 'It's nothing. Don't treat me like a child. It was something I ate, that's all.'

Amethyst did not know the reason for either of these signs of a nervous temperament, but gradually learned to cope with them. She could sense when a black mood was coming upon him and could now often turn it away before it overtook him. While he seemed to appreciate this, she sometimes felt he almost resented it as an intrusion upon his privacy.

'You are too good for me, my angel,' he would say, 'You bewitch me and understand me – perhaps too well.'

'How can I understand you *too* well? For God's

sake, Henry, why must you always be so private?'

'Because each of us, you, me, everyone, we all have some inner self . . . some secret part of ourselves that we do not wish to reveal. Something,' he would add, 'that perhaps we cannot reveal.'

Despite these low moments, their love affair did not waver and Amethyst felt that he trusted her increasingly – perhaps more than he had any other woman. She was thankful for this, and was relaxed enough to accept him as he was.

The door opened and at last he appeared, his figure elegant in his dinner jacket.

'I'm sorry I'm so late. I changed before telling you I'd finished the meeting, but here I am. You, my angel, look beautiful.'

He kissed her affectionately but as he ran his hands down the silken length of her she could sense his immediate surge of desire.

'Henry!' she laughed, 'one of the penalties about always being late is that it means we always have to go out as soon as you appear. And that means now.'

She kissed him cheerfully and with a last look in the mirror she picked up her evening bag and led him out of the room.

Chapter 2

Amethyst's mother still lived in Southsea, where Amethyst had spent all her life before she came to London. Her childhood had been like many others, marked only by the death of her father in a boating accident when she was ten. Amethyst had adored him, and he had worshipped her. It was clear from the beginning that she would take after her father in temperament as well as in looks. As Amethyst grew up she felt awkward and gauche beside her petite French mother. Amethyst loved the holidays they would go on to see their French relations, but her blondeness and height set her apart from her vivacious, chattering cousins more than did the language barrier, which she soon overcame.

Amethyst's parents had been married for some time before she was born. She would have loved to have had brothers and sisters, but her mother had told her this was not possible.

'Your mother had miscarriages – the babies were born too early and died – and she was very ill when you were born,' her father told her. The miscarriages had weakened Mariette and although not an invalid she was never really healthy. Mother and daughter were fond of each other but not too close; Amethyst blamed her mother's poor health, but the real reason for Mariette's reserve towards her daughter came from a feeling that from the moment Amethyst was born the child was the most important thing in her father's life.

Mariette had loved Gerald Barclay from the moment she met him. She had been working for some friends of his, looking after the four young children of the house, and had immediately admired the tall naval officer who came for the weekend. When guests were in the house she was expected to keep the children out of the way as much as possible, but luck was with her on this occasion as the weather was so fine that the whole party spent the days at the beach, and although naturally reserved, Mariette had managed to get into conversation with Barclay. He had been polite and friendly but did not seem to notice her particularly. He came to stay with the Wrights quite often that summer and was unfailingly kind to the lonely French girl. He was aware of her love for him but at first dismissed it as a crush. He did not realise the strength of character hidden behind the quiet exterior. Mariette had never seen her job as anything but an expedient. She was fond of children, but did not want to dedicate her life to looking after other people's. She wanted her own family. Mariette had not expected to fall in love with a friend of the Wrights – she was not included often enough in their social life to expect more than passing pleasantries from their acquaintances – but having fallen for Gerald Barclay she was determined to win him. She set her teeth, lifted her chin and promised herself that if she did not become Mrs Gerald Barclay it would be through no fault of her own. She made herself pretty and with every art she knew, from instinct and observation, she attracted Barclay to her. He was more lonely and vulnerable than he realised, and so Mariette won the only battle she undertook in her life.

Finally he married his virgin French bride. She wore white lace which did not suit her sallow skin and her head was full of dreams of endless babies and endless love. She was to some extent aware that his love for her was not as great as hers for him, but was sure she could change that. He had told her that he had had affairs – she would not have assumed otherwise – and that he had had one great love. In moments of jealousy towards that unknown woman Mariette would comfort herself with the thought that he could not have really have loved her more than herself. After all, it was Mariette he had married.

Years passed and she was forced to realise that she was not going to be blessed with five or six children. She found it fairly easy to conceive, but could never keep a child for longer than four months. Her obsessive desperation meant that her marriage was bound to suffer. Gerald had also wanted children, but his desire for them faded as he saw what was happening to his wife. He retreated into himself and became more and more prone to live in the past. He had left the Navy shortly after his marriage and began increasingly to regret it.

At last, after a pregnancy fraught with the terror of having yet another miscarriage, Amethyst was born and her parents' life was changed. Mariette listened to her doctors at last and decided she must be satisfied with what she had. Now she had given her husband the child that she had convinced herself he wanted more than anything, she was ready to turn back to him. But she had left it too late. Disappointed in his wife, Barclay had found consolation in the tiny baby. Years before it was fashionable Barclay took an active part in his daughter's upbringing and in her early childhood would hang over the nanny and try to take over even the dullest jobs.

'Come here and I'll do up your shoes and then we'll go down to the sea.' The child would put her small foot into her father's large hand and look up laughing.

'It's time for her rest.' The nanny always had some such protest but knew from experience that Barclay would have his way.

'Never mind a rest, the sea air will make her sleep all the better tonight. Come on, my jewel,' and he would swing her high onto his shoulders as she squealed with excitement.

Gerald Barclay's death in a boating accident when his daughter was only ten made several differences in Amethyst's life. Immediately after the first shock of overwhelming and terrifying grief, she was told that they were going to have to move house. Their joint grief had brought the mother and daughter closer then than they had ever been, but still Mariette had the very French attitude that children did not need too much explained to them.

'We are going to move. This house – it is too big now Daddy is dead. But we will still be in Southsea so nothing will change.'

Amethyst did not understand how her mother could be so obtuse. 'But Mum *everything* will change. What will happen to Billy?' Billy was a much loved and very dozy tortoise. She did not mean to sound selfish, but why couldn't her mother see that moving house was a change so basic that she would no longer be able to understand anything about the structure of her life. Furthermore, to move house but stay in the same town was a thousand times worse than to go somewhere completely new. Amethyst could not express her feelings adequately even to herself. Of course, in time she did overcome all the traumas. She continued to miss her father, but as she grew older she spent less time mourning him and, as children do, soon became used to his absence. She thought of him and felt a vague desire to do something that would have pleased him but as she had had so little knowledge of him, she could not really work out how he would have liked her to spend her life. All she knew for certain was she had no desire at all to become a WREN.

Amethyst always intended to go far in life, even before she knew which direction she would take. Above all she wanted independence, and with this in mind she took a Saturday job in a clothes shop as soon as she was able. She had self-discipline of a sort, but no academic discipline at all and so she left school with good enough A levels but no intention of going to university. This had caused endless discussion and much loss of temper.

'Of course you must continue with your studies – what are you thinking of?' Perhaps because she half believed her mother was in the right Amethyst felt constantly under attack and over-reacted whenever the conversation came up. But she wanted to 'get on with life' as she put it to herself, and did not want to waste three years in a provincial university studying something in which she had only a marginal interest. She also wanted to be able to earn money. School was over and from now on life was going to be an adventure.

The final solution was reached almost by accident. Amethyst heard someone mention that the local newspaper, the *Southsea Gazette*, had an opening for a trainee journalist. Amethyst had never considered writing as a career and was inclined to dismiss the term 'trainee journalist' as a way of describing an office dogsbody.

That evening one of the arguments about Amethyst's future flared up again. 'I want to be a journalist,' Amethyst said without stopping to think. 'The *Gazette* has an opening and I am going to see them tomorrow.' This was a blatant lie, and she was immediately made to feel guilty for it by her mother's support.

'But darling, that is wonderful. Why did you not tell me sooner? What could be better? And of course it would mean that you would still be with me. Now, my child, what will you wear to the interview?'

Surprisingly, Amethyst succeeded in being seen by the

editor the next day. Although apprehensive, she knew that the way to stand out was not to appear submissive, but gloriously self confident. Before the editor had had a chance to more than ask her name, Amethyst leapt in:

'It's very kind of you to see me, Mr Hunter. You see, I know I have no qualifications and I know nothing at all about the workings of journalism, but you see, I know that I'm going to be extraordinarily good at it, and I do think the *Gazette* is the right paper for me.' She paused for a moment to let her effrontery sink in and then laughed apologetically. 'I hired a video of *Front Page*.'

She got the job.

There are days in life which can never be forgotten. Amethyst's first day was one of these. Everything had gone smoothly for her till now. Although slightly reserved, she had been popular at school and as is perfectly normal, her last year had given her a certain amount of self-satisfaction. After a year of being thought glamorous by the younger children and being treated almost as an adult by the teachers, most people leave school thinking life is spread at their feet and there is nothing but enjoyment to come. Amethyst's wilfulness and her success at finding the job she said – and she convinced herself – she wanted, added to this. But when she arrived at the busy, smoky office where everyone seemed so sure of themselves she realised how far she had to go. A real job was very different from the fantasy. As Amethyst stood in the doorway at a complete loss she determined to do more than just become part of this scurrying mass of men whose names were automatic shortenings – Geoff, Tim, Dave, Alex – she would do more and go further. And she would do so without being called Ams or Ammy.

Everyone was friendly, if preoccupied, and gave her

small and mostly pointless jobs throughout that first day. Making the coffee and buying paperclips was called 'getting to know the ropes'. But suddenly she wanted to be part of it, to write, anything, even the local weddings.

Amethyst was subdued when she got home. Her mother was uncharacteristically excited and obviously proud. Amethyst tried to respond to Mariette's eager questioning. But what could she say? 'I made coffee all day?'

'And when will we see your name in print, *chérie*?'

'Oh, I won't get a by-line for ages.' Amethyst was pleased to have picked up some jargon at least. 'But when I know my way around a bit more I'll be put on to stories and then perhaps they'll let me write them up.' She laughed, thinking how long it would be before the Martians landed in Southsea or the police constable eloped with the headmaster of the local primary school.

Amethyst was soon accepted by the journalists who had seemed so awesome to her at first, and was friendly with most of them. As the only girl on the paper, she was treated with a mixture of respect and a rough equality. She soon enjoyed the flirting and teasing as much as the work.

After a short time she was sent off to report on local weddings and Women's Institute outings, with the promise of a feature when something came up. She began to take great glee in 'the bride wore cream chiffon trimmed with rosebuds. She was attended by Miss Charlene Williams and Miss Tracy Gazebee, who wore pink chiffon and the matron of honour was Mrs Louise Tilbury' (an eleven-stone divorcee with a whining child of five in tow) 'who wore peach chiffon.'

At first Amethyst's ideas for stories were either turned down or passed on to someone else to write up. She decided not to mind this, but to keep trying. She knew that some of her ideas were good and that given the chance she could write them as well as Geoff or Dave, and probably a lot better than Alex or Tim.

Then one day Jim Hunter, the editor, sent for her. He was a warm, straightforward man and easy to work for, but nevertheless it was not often she was called in to see him, and she felt as though she were on the way to see her headmistress as she tapped at his half-open door.

'Amethyst? Come in, love. I just want to remind you that your six months' probation with us is up.' She had forgotten that such a thing existed, and felt a surge of anxiety. 'We like having you around, so I'm giving you a rise and your three years' contract. Also I have a feature for you – not that exciting, but a start. The Miss Portsmouth Competition is next week and I want you to get an interview with her. Not that the world press will be competing, but who knows, she could be the next Miss England.'

'I doubt that – but I'll try and make the punters believe it.'

'That's the idea. Here are two press tickets. Enjoy yourself.'

Amethyst knew that this first feature was in the nature of a test. No one except Miss Portsmouth's rivals and her grandmother would have the slightest interest in the interview, but that was the essence of local journalism. In the event she wrote the piece well.

Amethyst's next idea was to start a woman's page on the paper. She spent some months alternating between pestering and persuading Jim, but at last the project was under way and it worked very well. The woman's page was solely Amethyst's responsibility which satisfied her immensely, and although she still had to spend much of her time reporting on the weddings and flower shows, she worked hard at the woman's page and often surpassed the limited needs of Southsea's womanhood.

For two and a half years Amethyst worked diligently and on the whole happily with the *Southsea Gazette*. She occasionally yearned to go beyond the narrow confines of Southsea and Portsmouth, but knew that to break her contract would ruin her journalistic career, if only because of union rules. The mornings spent in local courts, the afternoons spent at flower shows and Women's Institute parties, football matches and weddings went on and on, but Amethyst did not lose her ambition or her pleasure in her work. Her career took first place in her life. She continued to live with her mother, but although she took advantage of such social life as the area had to offer, she knew brighter and better things must wait for the future. Several men took her out, but Amethyst did not fall in love nor into bed.

Things changed towards the end of her last contracted year at the paper. Amethyst was reporting on the launch of a ship at Portsmouth. This would have been covered by the paper in any case, but was of particular interest on this occasion as a minor and unpopular member of the Royal family had come for the launch. The national press was always prepared to run a story denigrating this parvenue, so Amethyst went in the hope that there might be a scoop. The general public obviously had much the same idea, as the crowd was larger than normal on such occasions, but Amethyst had planned ahead and found herself a good vantage point from where she would be able to hear everything and her photographer would be able to see everything. Although it was a bitterly cold January morning, the crowd was in festive mood, laughing and joking while beating their hands together in a slow hand-clap as much to keep off the cold as to encourage the Princess to make her appearance. There were even a few Union Jacks being waved. Despite everything, the cheerfulness of the Portsmouth royalists raised Amethyst's spirits. The cold brought a pink tinge to her pale cheeks and made her eyes water slightly and look especially blue. Amethyst was then suddenly pushed hard and nearly lost her balance. At once she felt a hand catch her elbow, which steadied her again.

'Sorry to knock you around like that, but I was about to be swept away with the tide.' The speaker was a tall man with thick brown hair and serious eyes. His tweed suit was of good cut but appealingly shabby. He was very much the Londoner in the provinces. 'Which paper are you with?'

'The *Southsea Gazette*.' Amethyst wished she could say something more distinguished, but spoke straight out and grinned at him broadly. 'I'm the local girl.'

'I hadn't realised how awake the local populace was to the Princess's interest value,' he said.

'We read the *News of the World* too, you know. I'm Amethyst Barclay,' she added, feeling it was time he introduced himself.

'Dan Murray – with the *Chronicle* but really using this as an excuse to do a bit of research for the book I'm writing.'

Just then the big black limousine drove up and the very tall, very stately Princess waved graciously to the crowd, which responded with a cheer, polite rather than enthusiastic.

'For heaven's sake, they can do better than that,' muttered Amethyst, taking a few notes.

'You don't realise – they expect either a crown or horns,' said her new friend. 'Above all, they want something to go hideously wrong.'

'Well, don't we all?' she answered. 'Perhaps we could hire each other to throw tomatoes and create scoops.'

'We could.' He looked doubtful. 'On the other hand we could have dinner together.'

Amethyst was taken aback. She looked up at him and realised with a rush how attractive the man was. A tall dark stranger walking into her life – well, why not?

He sensed her hesitation. 'Come on, I won't bite and I hate to sound unromantic but this *is* on "exes".'

Amethyst laughed, feeling a little more relaxed. Fleet Street expense accounts were legendary in the newspaper world and she realised it was a considerate way of saying, 'It's just a dinner. It can be romantic if you want . . . or not. It's up to you.'

He said, 'Besides, I'm hungry, cold, miserable, bloody-well fed-up with ships and seagulls and the only thing that brightens up this miserable hole is you. Say no and I'll probably dive in after the ship.'

He had a haunted, hungry look that belied his obvious success, and at that precise moment he looked terribly vulnerable. It was probably a well-practised art, Amethyst thought. Then she decided she didn't care. She wanted dinner with this man. Maybe she wanted more than just dinner.

'OK. Dinner it is.'

At eight-thirty they were sitting at a table in the Crest Hotel. After two strong drinks in the bar Amethyst was feeling euphoric and knew she would enjoy herself. This encounter was indeed different from anything she had yet known. She hardly noticed the food, which was average, or the fact that she drank more than usual. She was completely carried away by Dan's eloquent charm, by the impression he gave of coming from a world that was much wider than Amethyst's, a world to which she longed to belong. Dan had travelled widely, but what really struck Amethyst was his unvoiced assumption that travel was normal, not extraordinary. He told her about South America, China and Bermuda until her head was spinning with the pictures he had painted, the wine she had

43

drunk and the warmth of his smile.

'But in the end I'm a Londoner,' he told her as he peeled a white peach for her. 'Don't you love it more than anywhere?'

'I don't know it that well. I feel as if I'm play-acting when I do go up, you know, being a tart in Soho and a millionairess in Mayfair.'

He chuckled. 'I'd like to join in your jaunts.'

She watched him dissect the fruit with precision.

'I hope to move up there soon, but first I must finish my contract in Southsea,' she went on. His stories had made her home town seem even more claustrophobic than usual, and she sighed. 'It's funny, when I was little I used to watch the ships leave and wish I was on them – they could be going anywhere and you needn't know where until they arrived.

'But now I really want to go to London – big city, bright lights, all that sort of thing.'

'What's to stop you?' It was his turn to watch as her even white teeth bit into the firm flesh of the fruit. She licked some juice from her lips and suddenly he realised how much he desired her.

'Nothing, once I've finished my contract. Except Mum – but she can't keep me down here for ever.'

'Would she want to?' He pushed away his coffee cup and signalled for the bill. Amethyst realised the evening was nearly over and an unexpected sadness dampened her waking desire. He would soon leave and that would be that. Amethyst had more than enjoyed this hint of the outside world, she had loved his references to countries so alien to her. She had easily fallen into a teasing flirtation with him and above all they had laughed together so much more than she had with anyone else she knew. As they left the hotel it was almost a shock to see the same familiar old street.

'I'll walk you home.' He took hold of her arm and she shivered with pleasure. A second later his arm was around her shoulders, holding her close to him and keeping her warm. They walked slowly under the street lights, hardly talking but enjoying each other as much as they had in their more exuberant moments. They reached Amethyst's front door and Dan let her go.

'I'll see you again?' It was barely a question.

'I expect so,' she answered lightly, but before she knew what was happening she was being kissed with more passion than she had yet known, and was blindly returning his kisses. After a while he stood back and Amethyst leant shakily against the door. He waited until she had unlocked the door and watched her go in. Both were smiling secretly as the door closed between them.

Dan courted Amethyst for the rest of the week. To Amethyst, Dan was the epitome of sophistication and glamour and by the end she was hopelessly in love. His gold-brown eyes, his tall, spare figure, combined with his gentle humour and his obvious talent as a writer completely bewitched her. For the first time her work began to suffer and when he returned to London she was left bemused at the depth of her feelings for him. Men had spent months trying to get her into bed. Dan had not even hinted at sleeping with her, but had aroused that desire in her for the first time. She could not believe he did not want her, but she had no idea what to do next. Perhaps he had been disappointed in her after their week together.

Dan did not keep her waiting long. After a few days of silence he rang her at work and asked if she would come up to London for the weekend. Amethyst longed to go but hesitated. She knew what would happen if she stayed with Dan. It had to happen sooner or later, but perhaps he was the one and this was the moment. She began to be more and more convinced that he was, and it was. But it would be on his territory, and that and the prospect of the moment itself terrified her. The sheer pleasure of hearing his voice decided her.

'Yes,' she said, firmly. 'Yes, I can.'

'Good', he said confidently, as though there had been no doubt in his mind. 'Actually I'm going to have to drag you along on a job.'

Drag? Amethyst drew in her breath. Me? Going on a Fleet Street story?

'A job?'

'Yeh, bloody boring book launch. Still, it's a freebee – bite to eat, few drinks.' His voice became suddenly professional. 'And, of course, you'll meet a few people too. Be nice to 'em, let 'em remember you, swop cards. Could all come in useful later on.'

She was touched, flattered, more than a little impressed. He didn't have to do that. But perhaps this was the way it was going to be.

'Waterloo. Six. Under the clock. I'll be wearing pink wellies and a carnation. *Be* there!'

She laughed. 'Six. I'll be there.'

'Amethyst?' His voice was suddenly and strangely tender. 'I'm really looking forward to seeing you.'

'Me too, Dan,' she replied. 'Very much.'

So they met at six, under the clock at Waterloo, and approximately three and a half hours later, with gentleness, tenderness and a great deal of skill, Dan took her virginity. The earth, however, did not move.

When, three months later, Amethyst finished her contract with the *Southsea Gazette*, Dan did not find it difficult to persuade her to come to London. It was, after all, what she had been working towards for the past few years. It was all the better that she should have Dan waiting for her, giving her not only moral but actual support. With his help, it was not long before Amethyst found a job on a weekly woman's magazine. She threw herself into the job with all her usual energy and determination. By now she knew how to set about her work and she knew what she wanted. For the first time a bright future seemed to be within reach and this gave her a sense of purpose. She enjoyed this job much more than she had her work in Southsea, but before the year was out she realised that it was in its way as limited as the old one. She decided that the answer was to become freelance but was still too unsure of herself to make the break.

Luck was once again on her side. After a year in London, she was asked at the last moment to take on a job far beyond her previous range.

'You speak French, don't you?' The question came out of the blue from her editor.

'Yes, quite well.'

'Quite well or better?' Amethyst realised something was up and decided not to undersell herself.

'Very well. My mother's French – I suppose I could call myself fluent.'

'Good. I want you to go to Paris tomorrow. Simon's got some bug and this interview's taken ages to set up. We can't afford to lose it, apart from which God knows how we'll fill the space if we let it go.' Although the magazine worked weeks ahead, there seemed to be a permanent frenzy as to how to fill the space.

Amethyst knew she should remember who Simon was going to interview but could not. 'Who am I to interview?' 'Mme Simone Veil, the French Transport Minister. A strong woman's story – should go down well. Ring Simon for details and perhaps you can take advantage of his research.'

Amethyst decided immediately not to take advantage of his research. This was her chance.

47

It was Amethyst's nature to do very well under pressure. This article was no exception. It succeeded even better than Amethyst had dared to hope. She discovered a talent that she never knew she had. On meeting Mme Veil she had felt nervous and on her mettle. She knew that this was her first real chance to prove herself. At the same time she realised that she had to appear relaxed and at ease. She did. Her confidence in her French was a great help and so, although she did not know it, were her wide blue eyes and confident air. It was only when she played back the tape that she realised quite how much Mme Simone Veil had been drawn out. There was the conventional and much repeated material about well-worn political issues, but Amethyst had also coaxed a discussion about the conflict between family life and a career and even the attitudes of ' *les hommes de nos jours*' to sex. All of which was very good magazine fodder and also more intimate and jokey than any other interview the minister had yet given.

The article gave Amethyst temporary fame, but it went further than that. Her editor now used her for nearly all the interviews, and they all gave the same impression of confidences having been exchanged between two people, rather than a journalist sitting down and firing a lot of questions at a celebrity. Amethyst's reputation grew, and she was approached by a few other women's magazines. She decided, however, that although she was working towards leaving the magazine, she would not leave it to go elsewhere, but to work on her own.

Meanwhile her affair with Dan was not going well. The first crack came when Amethyst bought her Maida Vale flat.

'I've got to have my own place, Dan. I mean, say you left me? Where would I be? Loverless and homeless. I've always wanted a flat – you knew that all along.'

His voice was bitter: 'Oh, it was a flat you wanted? Forgive me, I thought you already had a flat – the one you shared with me!'

She put a hand on his arm. 'Yes, Dan, I have a flat, and I've loved it here.' He noticed the past tense like the first symptom of an illness. 'But I need my own space, my . . . my own territory.'

'Territory? God, what is this? A Western?'

'Dan, try and understand. Yes, I need territory, somewhere I can retreat to and be alone. Everyone needs that, even you. I know I crowd you sometimes.'

'Oh, two's a crowd now, is it?'

She felt a surge of anger at him, at his narrowness, and at his unwillingness to understand. Then she suppressed it. This man had taught her a lot, given her a lot, and whatever she needed now she still cared for him a great deal.

'Just come and see it, Dan. It's right for me. Please.'

He shrugged. 'OK. What have I got to lose?' But he knew. What I have to lose, and will lose, Amethyst, is you, he thought, sadly.

Although she had denied it both to herself and to Dan, the move did make a difference to how often they saw each other. This gave her time to think, and she did not like the turn of her thoughts. She realised that her love for Dan had turned into a bland affection and that no element of passion remained. Then she began to wonder how much passion there had ever been. Had she fallen in love with Dan, or had he represented freedom and a means of escape? Looking back, she saw how naive she had been when they met in Southsea and knew that Dan was not the glamorous and sophisticated person she had imagined him. He was kind, funny, intelligent and talented but . . . It was no use repeating the list of his virtues to herself as some kind of charm. She no longer loved him.

The break was more painful than she had imagined it would be. She had thought that there would be one painful scene, a few tears, and then relief. She would be able to go out to dinner with other men without worrying at how attractive she found them. She could go or not go to parties without having to explain herself to anyone. She would be wholly and blessedly free, in her new home, with her own thoughts. Of course it was not like that. She felt guilty at having caused Dan so much unhappiness. She missed him enormously and would ring him up for a chat only to realise this made him more, not less, unhappy. She got depressed and careless at work.

'What's happened to the jokey old Amethyst?' a friend said to her at a publisher's party. 'The wine's foul and the book's appalling, but life isn't that bad. You need a holiday. Anthony and I are going to Jamaica to live the life of the idle rich for a few weeks. Why don't you come too? Five of us are going at the moment so you'll make up the numbers.'

'I couldn't, Molly. What about work?' Amethyst protested, but the protest was only half-hearted.

'Don't be silly. I bet you've not missed a day since you started. Be brave – just come. Look, there's Anthony. Come on, he'll talk you into it.'

The next day Amethyst woke up early feeling happier than she had for weeks. Then she remembered why. She reached out for the telephone and dialled Molly.

'Did you mean it? Can I really come?'

'Amethyst? Of course you can. Let's have lunch and make plans. I'll meet you in 'Escargot at one.' Amethyst heard a sleepy mutter. 'Anthony says he's over the moon.'

'He sounds like a sleepy footballer. Make sure when he wakes up he realises it's not a dream. See you at one.' Laughing and feeling incredibly light-hearted she put the

50

receiver down. Life was looking up again.

Amethyst was finding it hard to believe that such a way of life existed. Molly had talked of aping the idle rich, but Amethyst had no idea quite how idle or how rich these people were. Within a week of accepting the invitation she was lounging in the sun, drinking endless multi-coloured cocktails from long cold glasses and changing every evening into her most elegant and expensive dresses. They were staying with friends of Anthony's, and Molly had vaguely warned Amethyst of the life-style.

'It'll cost nothing to be there,' Molly had said that day as they sat in 'Escargot. She looked greedily at the warm pigeon breast salad that the waiter was putting in front of her. 'But you will need a few clothes.'

'I was hoping for a bit of lazy beach life.' Amethyst's appetite had returned and she attacked her own shredded duck happily.

'Oh, there'll be that all right, but there'll be parties and they change every night for dinner – black tie rather than a clean shirt. And you can't really wear the same dress more than once.'

Even then Amethyst had not really taken in what the holiday would be like. She had a therapeutic, very enjoyable and highly expensive shopping spree and set off for the sun. Anthony's friends were charming and although young and blithe seemed like people from another century with their languorous way of life and polished etiquette. Jim's parents had owned coffee plantations and had built wisely on their money; the son had made a career out of enjoying himself. Lucy, his wife of less than a year, was a very pretty white Jamaican with a strong West Indian accent, which surprised Amethyst although she later found out that this was typical. She

51

took to Lucy immediately and the girls spent a lot of time swimming in the limpid blue pool and soaking up the wealth of sunshine.

The days were long and they kept late hours, eating at ten, before going on to a club or staying in, just drinking or dancing on the terrace. The men dressed in dinner jackets despite the heat, and the women in brilliantly coloured gowns of chiffons and taffetas, with bare shoulders and backs. They would gather together at the end of the day looking suntanned and ridiculously fit, drinking champagne from Lalique crystal or yet another of the butler's imaginative cocktails before moving into the long cool dining room. Every night the dinner table glittered with laughter and fine Georgian silver. The Asprey jewels dazzled on bare shoulders in the candle-light and everyone's eyes seemed larger and the atmosphere full of heavenly glamour. Before dinner every night Jim would solemnly toast the Queen and the company would rise and drink to the monarch. The first time this happened Amethyst was taken completely by surprise and had to bite her cheeks to hold back a giggle. It just could not be true. Molly caught her eye and pulled a quick face at her before drinking with mock seriousness. Afterwards, while the men were still sitting in the dining room and the women were lazily rocking on the terrace, Molly apologised.

'I should have warned you. It caught me on the hop the first time too. They do it every night.'

'Is it just Jim or everyone here?'

'I don't know. They've certainly toasted her everywhere I've been.'

'Do you think when Jim and Lucy are eating an omelette on their own they solemnly drink her health in plonk?' Amethyst's repressed giggles suddenly broke out as she pictured the scene. Do they ever eat in the kitchen? Probably not . . .

The stylised colonial life fascinated and amused Amethyst, and she became very fond of Lucy and Jim and the rest of the house party, but after a week she began to feel the need for some kind of a change. Lying on the beach reading Patrick Leigh Fermor's *The Traveller's Tree* she suddenly remembered having heard that Jamaica was the one place in the West from where there are direct flights to Cuba. On the spur of the moment she decided to go there for a few days by herself, and by the next evening, having made apologies to her host and hostess and promised to be back within a week, she had checked into the Hilton hotel in Havana.

From the moment she arrived in Cuba she loved it. The heat was almost unbearable in its subtropical steaminess, but the hotel was well air-conditioned and all the buildings she went into were cool enough. She spent the first day walking around Havana, amazed at how different it was from anything she knew. She strolled through the tropical gardens, admiring the dense green foliage and the brightly coloured flowers. That evening she went to bed early feeling completely relaxed and rejuvenated. The Cubans seemed a friendly people and everyone she had come across was helpful. On the second day, she went to a sugar factory, and found she was allowed a brief tour around the works. Amethyst had imagined Cuba as a totally deprived and seedy country, and was therefore pleasantly impressed by the good working conditions. She found that Havana had a very good crêche system, as most families had two working parents, and she visited a day care centre. It suddenly seemed like a good idea to spend some time researching as far as she could into the daily lives of the Cubans. While she had no definite plans to write an

53

article, Amethyst felt that she would enjoy her stay more if she was working towards something.

By the end of the day she needed some more social pastime. Although by now totally independent and fearless, she had never got used to sitting on her own in bars for any stretch of time. But now she had no alternative. Even then, she told herself, she could pretend that she was working. She showered and changed and after dinner in the hotel set off for the Tropicana, ready to enjoy a drink and watch the company as well as the showgirls. She had decided to see if she could sense a Russian presence, and thought that a night-club would be a good place to start looking.

She sat at a corner table, drinking brandy and coffee and watching everyone around her. She liked the feeling that she was unknown and on her own, and for the moment felt completely happy alone. No one seemed to be in uniform. Everyone was there to have a good time; there appeared to be no heavy discussions going on under the cover of the music.

Amethyst had been there for about three-quarters of an hour and was beginning to think about leaving when a waiter appeared with a bottle of brandy on a tray.

'The gentleman on table 23 has sent you this, Señorita,' he murmured as she started to protest. She followed the direction of his gesture and saw an immaculately groomed man bowing to her from across the room. He was certainly in a different league from the men she had seen and talked to during the day.

'He says, may he join you for a drink?' Amethyst was about to refuse and send the bottle away but then she thought better of it. Why not, after all? He was handsome and she was on holiday. She had spent the day researching into working Cubans and now she could talk to a playing

Cuban. She returned the stranger's smile and nodded slightly.

'Could you bring another glass?' she asked the waiter, who bowed and disappeared.

Her suitor was standing over her as soon as the waiter left. His good looks were obvious and very Latin and Amethyst warmed immediately to his smile. Only minutes earlier she had been congratulating herself on her self-sufficiency, but now she was more than happy to have company.

'You are English?' His accent was heavy, but he seemed sure of his command of the language.

'Yes.' She would not introduce herself first; she thought that that was up to him.

'I saw you were alone, and so was I. It seemed such a waste.' She had never thought she would be so easy to pick up.

'May I sit down?'

'Of course.' She gestured at the place opposite her and smiled.

'Juan Pedro Diaz. I knew I would not be able to sleep and decided to come here for company. Little did I know how lucky I would be.' Amethyst began to think that perhaps his charm was too self-conscious and would soon become oppressive, but he fell silent as the waiter brought him a glass and poured them both coffee. When he spoke again he seemed more at ease. 'What are you doing in Cuba? So you are not a Yankee, but English, yes?' He flashed a brilliant Latin smile.

'English . . . and minding my own business.' She smiled back, a London social smile, patently insincere.

'You have business in Cuba?' He looked puzzled then his eyes twinkled. 'Ah, I understand.' He tapped his nose. 'You say I am being what you English call nosey . . . that I put it where I should not.' He laughed, and this time it seemed sincere. Amethyst warmed to him. This was no pompous Latin lover but a man with a real sense of humour.

She said: 'Actually, that was rude of me.' She put out her hand, and the man took it. She said: 'I'm Amethyst and I'm in Cuba because . . . I felt like coming. I was in Jamaica being bored rigid by a lot of too rich, too fat Brits and I needed some fresh intellectual air. Cuba seemed to be the place. Does that answer your question, Señor . . .?'

'Diaz. Yes, it does. You are here because you are a communist?' She noted the faintest hint of hostility in his voice now, a sort of hardening of tone. She wondered why.

'My politics are my business. As it happens, I am not a communist. Should I be?'

'You may be what you wish. I just wish your country, and America particularly, took the same view of us.'

She probed. 'But do you not get communists here, people from Europe?'

He sipped at his drink. 'Yes, we do. I should like them, I know. They are Cuba's friends, they speak up for us against the United States, they . . .' He shrugged.

'But you don't?'

He was silent for several seconds. Then he said: 'The English come and are very dull and very earnest. They pat us on the back and tell us they wish their country was like ours. Then they go back to their cars, their big houses and washing machines and TV sets. They do not really know what Cuba is about.'

He gave a small helpless moue. Amethyst was intrigued.

'Just the English?'

He seemed to snap out of his mood. 'Oh no. But the

56

English are the best. You should see our Italian comrades. They simply will not eat Cuban food. The French, well . . . by far the best dressed, and by far the most snobbish. I think French communism comes with a designer label.'

Amethyst laughed out loud. 'You've forgotten the . . .'

'The Russians? Of course not.' His expression was suddenly serious. 'Without them we would be a Yankee colony, make no mistake.' He put his hand to his mouth as though imparting a secret that must not be overheard. 'But that doesn't mean that I'd want to get into bed with one. They are so ugly.' He laughed again, that genuine, unaffected laugh that Amethyst was beginning to find so attractive. 'And they only have fun when they get drunk.'

'OK then, I'm not a Euro-Communist and I'm not a Russian. Does that mean I am welcome in Cuba? Just who do you like?'

He took another long sip of his drink and looked her directly in the eye. 'I like – *Cuba* likes – those who would come here and take us for what we are. Who would not patronise us, would not destroy us or wish to make us a colony. Who would wish to help us when we need help. Those who . . .' He paused. 'What was your name?'

'Amethyst. Amethyst Barclay.'

Half to himself he said, 'A precious stone . . .' Then, 'Amethyst we welcome those who come to us in peace and with a spirit of enquiry, who would leave Cuba enriched by having been here, and Cuba a little richer for their presence, who would go into the world and tell them that we are people, not a collection of ideologies.'

Amethyst lifted her coffee. '*Salud*. You should be a poet.'

'Ah,' he said, gravely. 'I *am* a poet, as many Cubans

57

are, but I also run the state tobacco plantations in the East.'

The next hour passed incredibly quickly. Diaz was a mine of information, cultural, political, historical, social, about his country, and when Amethyst professed her ignorance of the National Ballet of Cuba, he raised his eyebrows in mock affront.

'You do not know of the National Ballet of Cuba?' he exclaimed, only half pretending to be shocked. 'We are so very proud of it. Indeed, it went to London about a year and a half ago.'

'I must have missed it.' Amethyst was secretly amused. Now that she had been reminded she did remember Suzy Porter complaining loudly about a very old prima ballerina who had actually fallen over. She decided it would be tactless to bring that up.

'More important, and perhaps as beautiful in a different way, are our cattle farms,' Juan continued. 'Fidel takes great pride in them, as we all do.' Amethyst noticed the use of the Christian name and was curious. If she had fallen in with someone who knew Castro, she could perhaps get something interesting from him. She sipped her brandy and soda thoughtfully.

'Perhaps you would like to come and see one of our ranches?' he asked. 'As a journalist you would perhaps be interested?'

'I'd be *very* interested. But I must leave Havana in the next few days.' She was determined not to make vague plans which would never be fulfilled.

'Tomorrow I will ring Raoul and will call you. It would be a pleasure to take you.'

Raoul. That was a coup. Of course, Raoul was a common enough name, but she was sure she was being taken to see Castro's brother who ran the state cattle farms. Amethyst believed Juan would keep his word and would at least try to take her, and she spent the rest of the evening deliberately charming him with her humour, her dancing and her Anglo-Saxon looks. She was looking forward to her outing and would sing for her supper.

The next day Juan took Amethyst out to lunch and early in the evening they set off in his car towards the state farm at Colorro.

Amethyst was thoughtful as she was shown the huge bulls and the fine herds of cattle. She could not at first understand how the barns stayed so cool in spite of the oppressive heat outside. Then she became aware of a familiar whirring in the background. Juan was watching her as she looked up and saw a machine she recognised fixed high up on the wall.

'Yes, you've noticed.' He smiled, like a teacher pleased with his pupil.

'Air-conditioning?'

'Sure,' said Raoul. 'These bulls represent a massive investment on behalf of our people, so we spoil them a little.' He pointed out a particularly fine bull and said, 'That one is English. Like you,' he added with a smile. 'I bought him at your Royal Show. I go most years to buy and compare.' How many journalists knew that? Amethyst wondered. After a while she excused herself from the men, who were discussing some minor problem with a farm hand, and walked over to the ranch office. There she found only a dark handsome woman who introduced herself as Maria and invited her and Juan for dinner at her home in Havana. Amethyst sat down with Maria on the verandah and accepted a cold drink.

As they talked, Maria gave her a warm smile and Amethyst felt a sudden urge to confide in this striking woman.

'Maria,' she said, 'I have become very interested in your country.' She waited for hostility. She knew by now how Cubans felt about the media, and their invariable distrust.

'But of course you have,' Maria said. She expected no less from anyone who visited her native land.

'I know next to nothing about Cuba, or Fidel, or your history, or what your people think and believe. And why there is so much hostility from the rest of the world.' Amethyst suddenly faltered, embarrassed by her own enthusiasm.

Maria laughed generously. 'Only the Yankee propaganda, eh? That's all you know, like most people. We are all soulless Marxists who threaten the United States.' Her voice quickened with anger. 'Can a gnat threaten an elephant? And Fidel is the worst victim of these lies. If only they knew, if they could only understand . . .'

So Maria talked and Amethyst listened, fascinated by the passion of Maria's convictions. She talked of Fidel Castro with an emotional strength that was almost that of a woman defending her lover. Perhaps, Amethyst thought. And why not? Maria talked about her country, pouring out her innermost feelings, giving up the core of herself to Amethyst, and in return the English girl felt the need to unburden too, to give in return, and almost without knowing it, she was talking, the woman Maria questioning gently, encouraging her to talk more and more. Amethyst talked of Dan and their relationship; about how she felt, what she needed and wanted. There, in the sultry Cuban night, it was like a release to pour this out to a sympathetic stranger – one she would probably never see again.

They saw Raoul and Juan on their way back. A convoy of army trucks was approaching at high speed. They drew to a halt beside the terrace. Amethyst could not see who got out but Maria's face lit up. As a figure detached itself from a mass of armed guards, Amethyst could not believe her luck. The thick beard and the huge frame in green army fatigues were unmistakable. The unexpected beauty of the eyes and the low rasping quality of the voice made this man more attractive than she would have imagined. As he kissed Maria and held her hands for a second, Amethyst wondered how she could have been so slow. Of course Maria must be Castro's lover. This was why she was so fierce in her loyalty to him. Castro himself was charming to Amethyst. He immediately accepted her as a friend of Juan's and sat next to her on the terrace. She was soon completely won over and a little bit in love with him herself. This was no dictatorial ogre. He was a warm and very flirtatious human being. She soon found herself as convinced as Maria and Raoul that events had been against him, and that he was serving his country with loyalty and as best he could. The bushy beard and the delicious aroma of his Cohiva cigars were all that fitted with her preconceived notions of the Cuban leader.

Over the next days Amethyst spent some time with Maria, and saw Castro and Raoul again. While she regarded the week as a holiday, she knew that her talks with Maria had been invaluable and that she could not let the chance of writing about them go by. On her last evening she had dinner with Juan and Maria. By now she was on terms of easy familiarity with them both, and was sorry to be leaving to go back to the effete way of life in Jamaica.

At the end of the meal she took Maria aside.

'You've been so open with me; in turn I've told you things that I've never really discussed so openly with anyone.'

Maria took her arm. 'Woman to woman. Truth. It never hurts.'

'Yes, I know, so I want you to understand that I will have to write about Cuba when I return to England. Write about you, Raoul, Fidel . . . the things I've seen.'

Maria gave her a quick hug. 'You must write. You have seen us, eaten with us, you have seen the way we are, not what others say we are. Just write the truth as you saw it; you can do no other. And Amethyst, when you write of the one who is so important to Cuba . . . so dear to me . . . When you write of him, be extra careful with your truth. Give no one ammunition to harm him more.'

Amethyst returned the hug. 'Maria, I shall write what I saw – and I will never forget you.'

The woman smiled warmly. 'Just write what you saw and Cuba will never forget you.'

Amethyst could not wait to get to a typewriter.

Amethyst's article on Cuba had more impact than she would ever have thought possible. Her acquaintance with Castro gave the article a rare insight: she wrote a well-balanced portrait of a man, not a eulogy of a public figure. She mentioned his affection for Maria and put into perspective his relationship with America, reminding people how he had been rejected twice. The story was sold to a syndicate and published worldwide, along with photographs Amethyst had taken while on the ranch. Amethyst was already known for the authentic quality of her interviews, but the intimacy of the article about Fidel Castro was unheard of at that time.

The article brought her more than simply personal success. To her amazement she found herself rung up by an American from the embassy in Grosvenor Square who took her to lunch at the Ritz. Halfway through the lobster she realised that an important diplomat was actually asking her opinion on how America should approach Cuba. He could not have been more circumspect in the way he put the questions, but that was nevertheless the essence of what he was saying. Not long afterwards a small group of American senators went on what was called a fact-finding tour to Cuba. A mild thaw set in between Uncle Sam and his errant nephew in the backyard.

At last Amethyst's talent was paying off and now she opted to go freelance. She was greatly in demand and could ask large fees for her interviews and features. She was everything modern woman aims for: independent, talented, successful and attractive. It was her spirit of independence that had first attracted Sylvia to her when they had originally met in New York: her independence, but also the rarely-indulged feeling of loneliness which Sylvia had sensed in her. Sylvia determined to find her protégée a life and lover that would banish her occasional wistfulness. So as soon as she had noticed Amethyst's thinly disguised interest in Brauner at that first meeting she had made every effort to bring her two friends together.

The old Jew was easy. He was half-blind now, unsteady on his feet, hearing impaired. Only his memory was really intact, and that could not save him. Indirectly it was what would kill him. He was two feet from the kerb, crossing the cobbled road diagonally and could only sense the battered, black Mercedes seconds before it hit him.

There was time for a small cry, an exclamation of surprise and fear, then just the impact of steel on fragile bones, the long, slow descent into blackness. The few who rushed to the body lying in the gutter, the blood seeping into the dust, could not understand why the old man died with a soft smile on his face.

Someone swore too that before he whispered Sh'ma Israel, *the holiest of the Jewish prayers, he had said another word that had no religious significance. It was 'Check-mate'.*

They took the agent at four in the morning. Four carloads of plain-clothes Vopos, a sledge-hammer on the door of the small apartment, and then the young man was dragged from his bed, cuffed, punched and manhandled naked into the back seat of an unmarked Wartburg.

In a small basement room beneath the Volkspolizei *barracks in Molotov Strasse they beat him efficiently, silently, with fists and boots, while he screamed and pleaded for mercy, promisiing that nothing had been passed on. They took him to the large, square room with the big bath and the hand-cranked generator. Someone put on a tape of appalling Russian pop music. Someone else attached the electrodes to his nipples, ears and genitals.*

Then another began the questioning.

He did not change his story; instead he wept and begged for his life.

It was his cowardice that finally convinced them, and they left him alone for ten minutes, shocked, hurt and shivering in a small cell, while they conferred, and telephone calls were made. His entreaties, his whimpering cries reached down the corridor to the smoky office that smelled of Russian cigarettes.

At length the cell door opened again, and the man looked up. There were three Vopos in uniform, hard men with cropped skulls beneath their peaked caps.

Two pinned his arms, forced him to his knees, swivelled him and bent his head until it was inches from the stone floor.

They stepped back and left him kneeling like a supplicant.

The third Vopo took an automatic pistol from his leather holster, cocked it carefully, took a pace forward and shot the kneeling man through the back of the neck.

There are different kinds of courage. Perhaps the greatest is to endure pain and torture, then to die at an executioner's hand, appearing to those who torment you like a coward to the last.

As he had knelt, cold, bruised and hurting, seconds from death, he whimpered and pleaded, keeping up the act until the end. His only satisfaction was that far away, in a sunnier land, the land of his people, someone would know that he was not a coward but a brave man. For he had beaten them. The message was over, passed quickly to a visiting businessman, by now already being decoded in Tel Aviv. He had beaten them. Through the tears there was fire and triumph in the bruised eyes.

He mouthed the Sh'ma Israel: 'Hear, O Israel, the Lord our God, the Lord is One,' and died.

The telephone line between Leipzig and Moscow crackled with interference, and the German had trouble with the Russian's heavy accent.

'Are you sure there can be no link?'

'Bitte?'

'No one can know?'

'No. The Jew told only this amateur, and we are sure he passed on nothing. He has no radio, no known courier and he had the information for twenty-four hours only. We questioned him thoroughly and carefully.' The Russian knew exactly what that meant.

'Even in the bathroom he did not change what he said. He was a coward too, that was plain. If he knew anything he would have told us, if it meant him getting out of the bathroom.'

'I thought these men trained their Jews better?'

'He was new to the game. It showed.'

65

'It's closed?'

'Completely. Whatever information this was . . .' there was irony in the German's voice. He had not been privy to what exactly was supposed to have been passed on '. . . whatever it was lies in the quicklime with the two Jews who held it.'

The Russian registered approval from Dherzinsky Square. 'Good. Krellmer?'

'Yes, Colonel?'

'You have done well. It will not go unnoticed. You have a promotion in the offing?'

'Indeed.'

'It will be accelerated. An improvement also in your living conditions, perhaps.'

The receiver was replaced, and the German looked out through the streaked window across to the spires of the old town. *For killing two Jews the USSR will make me a captain, and probably get me a better flat.*

The man laughed. In 1945 they had shot his father for doing more or less the same thing.

They waited two weeks after the message was deciphered. Two weeks for the agent to surface. Then news of his disappearance into the Vopo barracks reached them. The only conclusion was that the man was now dead. The news of the old Jew's death was almost a formality. So if the Israelis had been in any doubt about the authenticity of the bizarre news it was banished now.

A pistol shot in a damp cellar, an old man bleeding and broken in an East German gutter. Two signatures on the most stunning and dangerous message the State of Israel had ever received.

PART TWO

DAVID

Chapter 1

The man came out of the cool of the Sheraton's air-conditioning into the heat of Hayarkon Street. He felt himself blink in the Mediterranean glare. Gripping the handle of the attaché case, he dodged through the traffic, and walked fifty yards up the opposite side of the street to the King David Travel Agency. His appointment was for 2 pm and it was 1.57 exactly.

The travel agency was like hundreds of others scattered along the length of Hayarkon Street. A grimy glass-fronted office, festooned with faded ads for car-hire companies, tours to the Negev and Jerusalem, long weekends in Eilat; and inside a single fan moved the warm air around the room, ruffling the piled sheets of paper. A bored-looking man behind the counter looked up as the American came in, and said in English: '*Shalom*. You want to book a tour?'

'Normally,' the American said carefully, 'but this time I think I'd like to drive myself.'

The man straightened; his eyes became alert.

He said: 'What kind of car would you have in mind?'

'A Mercedes.'

The man pressed a button on a small plastic intercom and said in Hebrew: 'The man for the Mercedes is here.'

Then, to the American, in English, he added: 'Come with me, I think we might have what you are looking for.'

The two walked through to the back of the shop, through a side-door, down a long corridor, up a flight of

69

stairs, to a closed door. The Israeli stopped and knocked. Above them a small camera bolted to the wall glared down fixedly with its one eye.

A voice from nowhere said in Hebrew: 'Insert.'

The Israeli took what looked like a small credit card from his shirt pocket and slid it into a slit in the door. There was a short pause, and the American yawned. He always felt the Israelis were a trifle theatrical. The door opened and they stepped into the gloom. When the American's eyes adjusted he saw two hard-looking men staring at him, and a corridor stretching behind them. Further down, a third man leant with deceptive casualness against another door.

One of the men put out a hand and took the briefcase. 'Credentials,' he ordered.

The American reached into his pocket for an embossed card and handed it over. The man held it up to another camera fixed to the wall. There was a small 'ping' noise and the man handed back the card. He then opened and searched the briefcase, and frisked the American thoroughly, the expert hands feeling around the genitals and between the cleft of the buttocks without embarrassment. The second man produced a metal detector and ran it over the American's body from head to toe and then over the briefcase.

The American smiled to himself. Theatrical or not, no one trusted anyone else's spies, even if they were on the same side.

At last he was led down the corridor; a door was opened. He blinked in the light, then saw a man in his sixties, hand outstretched.

The man from the CIA shook the hand of the head of Mossad, the Israeli Secret Service.

★ ★ ★

The CIA man said: 'Our consent comes from the highest level.'

'You are sure you cannot deal with it yourselves?'

'Absolutely. I'd terminate the bastard myself if I could, but it is politically impossible for us even to be thought to be connected. You have anyone in mind for this? You know how delicate it is, there must be no slip-ups.'

'I have the man. He's the finest.'

'Good.' The American paused. 'I am authorised to say that the fact you told us about this is appreciated. It will result in future goodwill.'

The head of Mossad was more pleased than he dared show. 'It will result in future goodwill.' Six words, a bland phrase, but it could mean the difference at some moment in his country's future between survival and extinction. It could mean massive injections of cash, or secret shipments of arms or spare parts, in the event of some anti-Zionist embargo by Congress; it could mean leaked intelligence secrets, it could mean that extra edge to Israel's defence that she needed.

'Thank you.'

'For what?' The American pulled a wry grin. 'You could have been forgiven for just eliminating him yourselves without telling us.'

'On your territory . . . Charles.'

'Since when did national boundaries bother the Mossad?'

'No.' The Israeli spy chief shook his head emphatically. 'On this occasion you had to know, and approve. You had to see the evidence for yourself, otherwise I do not believe that any amount of it after the event would have convinced you.'

The American shrugged. 'Yes. I've been in the spook

business all my life and I've seen nothing like this. If I didn't know, hadn't seen the evidence, I wouldn't have believed it.'

David Avrim said: 'Why me?'

'Because you are the best. I was in Jerusalem yesterday. After the mission was approved the Prime Minister himself suggested your name.'

'The best don't make mistakes.'

'It was not your mistake. You were given the target and you eliminated it.'

'But an innocent man *is* dead.'

'Yes; one of many, Jew and Arab alike, who have died and will die before Israel is allowed to live in peace.'

'I have eleven months to go. I thought, somehow, that after . . . after what happened . . . I would be allowed to graze quietly.'

The Mossad chief looked at the fit, bronzed young man before him. A man talking of retirement, yet just thirty-six in eleven months' time. After that date no man was thought fit, or mentally alert, enough to be a Mossad field agent.

'What will you do then? Stay on the moshav full-time?'

David Avrim's eyes brightened. 'Yes, I like being a farmer and I think I'm not quite gregarious enough to be a kibbutznik, but the moshav suits me. I've had my bellyful of towns and cities. Paris, Rome . . . Tel Aviv.'

The older man smiled.

'In the meantime? You are under Mossad orders, but, of course, I would not dream of ordering someone to do something like this, not if they felt, or *I* felt their heart was not in it. It will be your last job, your last task for your country, your most important.'

'My last job.' David bit his lip. 'I remember Yuri

72

Moscowitz's last job. A routine trip into Damascus, four days at most, one meet, he'd done it half a dozen times before. Only this time he ended up in a cellar with his balls cut off, eyes gouged out, longing for the mercy of a pistol shot.'

'As I said, David, I shall not force you. Perhaps, though, it is a moment to redeem yourself, not in our eyes, but your own.'

David stayed silent.

'Will you do it?'

'Yes. Now tell me. Who is it? Who am I to eliminate and why?'

The Mossad chief told him the whole story, leaving nothing out.

'It is almost beyond belief.'

'Almost, but not quite. We have spent twelve months checking this. It is quite true. The Americans have double checked, and they too know it to be true. We have Charles Langley's permission to operate on their territory.'

'The girl?'

'Is not to be harmed. And David . . .' the Mossad chief looked hard at him and there was a sharp, dangerous tone to his voice '. . . your reputation as a lover is only exceeded by that as an agent.'

David smiled thinly. 'Is that praise?'

'It is a warning. In the matter of the girl there will be nothing between you. Nothing romantic or sexual. She is business only. Do I make myself clear?'

'Absolutely. But why?'

'Look on it as a religious prohibition. For the Mossad is your religion and I am your rabbi, and I am telling you. Nothing with the girl. *Nothing*. Do I make myself clear?'

'For the second time – absolutely. She probably has buck teeth and acne.'

'Back to business, David. Where, when . . . and more importantly, how.'

Chapter 2

It was the day when David would become a man, the day and the ceremony that would take him across the threshold away from childhood and its innocence into adulthood, its mysteries and its fears and possibilities.

Like all Jewish boys he had at last come to the day of his Bar Mitzvah, the ceremony for which he had been preparing for months, the moment that the law of his religion and race decreed he would, at last, become a man.

At Kefar Habad, an ultra-orthodox farming community not far from Tel Aviv, the service in the synagogue that sunny April of 1961 seemed much as usual. Yet for some reason there was an air of anticipation that lent importance to the occasion. Long black official-looking cars lined the driveways and many of Israel's familiar political faces were to be seen in the congregation. Perhaps it had something to do with the fact that all the boys taking their Bar Mitzvah today had lost a father or mother fighting for Israel in the War of Independence.

David Avrim had lost both parents, but having been brought up on the kibbutz that they had died defending he did not feel, and was not allowed to feel, different from the other children – the communal upbringing meant that all children were automatically treated the same. David was a good-looking and intelligent child, remarkable for the bright, greeny-blue eyes in his tanned, handsome face. He was proud of the fact that his parents had died defending Kibbutz Kinnerett in the War. As soon as he understood the reasons for their deaths – which took place before he was old enough to have any memory of either of them – he swore that he too, above all, would defend his country. His 'uncle' Aaron Dulitski, who did not live on the kibbutz but was his guardian throughout his childhood, smiled at those first childish protestations.

'There is time, David. We shall see.'

'You will see, Uncle Aaron,' the child would declare, clenching his small fists and tilting his head so that he could fix his solemn green eyes on his uncle's face. 'I have no family but Israel. When I am big enough I shall fight for her. You will see.'

Now, without telling anyone, even his closest friend Joshua or his uncle Aaron, he had resolved to use his Bar Mitzvah to show them his serious intent.

On that Sabbath morning, David was reassured to see his uncle Aaron. Dulitski had arrived with several important looking men and women. David was surprised to see the number of well-known politicians among them, but everything was surprising on this all-important day.

Before the service started, Dulitski found an opportunity to take David aside and give him a few words of comfort and encouragement.

'You are soon to be a man, David. I have been proud to be your guardian until now. When you are a man I shall be your friend.'

David adopted his manly stance, an arrogant straightening of his back which would stay with him for the rest of his life.

'You will always be proud of me, Uncle Aaron. I will be a man for Israel.'

Dulitski was momentarily taken aback, but could not

be but pleased at his ward's apparent devotion to the course to which he had always dedicated his life. He turned towards the two adults who stood by him.

'This is the child – David Avrim – of whom I spoke to you.'

'A war orphan,' the smaller of the two men, greying and with an intense look partly caused by the fact that he had lost his right eye some years before, stated rather than asked.

'Yes. His mother was Ruth Avrim.'

'Ah yes. His father?'

'His father.' Dulitski seemed to hesitate.

David spoke up. 'My father died for Israel with my mother on Kibbutz Kennerett in 1948.' He spoke with pride.

A quick look passed between the adults. David was now abashed, thinking he had perhaps been too forward.

'Your father – yes, I remember.' Dyan's look was kind. 'Go back to the others, David. God be with you.' Dulitski echoed the blessing and David rejoined his fellows, trembling now with growing excitement over his initiation into Jewish manhood.

At last the service was over, and that evening there was a party in the hall for the Bar Mitzvah boys. Dulitski had given David a camera as a gift, and David could not wait to start testing it out. He was thanking his uncle for the present when the time came for him to give a short speech of thanks to the community of Kefar Habad for inviting the boys to celebrate their Bar Mitzvah with them.

David stepped forward to say his words. This was the moment he had been waiting for. He felt his palms sweat as he took the microphone. He spoke the few simple words of thanks expected of him, and the company clapped politely. Then he braced himself. In a clear voice he began another speech he had written himself.

'People believe,' he said, 'that because I am an orphan I have no family. But that is not true. Israel is my family. She has given me the warmth of a mother's love and the guidance of a father. I promise in my manhood to serve her with strength and devotion.' The hall was silent as David added, 'I pledge to honour her as a faithful son all the days of my life.'

There was a general intake of breath at the melodramatic words and the intense air. The boy was little more than a child, but was obviously sincere, not seeking attention.

Afterwards, Dulitski found David and kissed him on both cheeks. 'What made you say that?'

'I've planned it for some time, Uncle Aaron. I know it will be years before I can join the army, but until then I will study. Perhaps one day there will be no more fighting.'

David was not completely sure why he felt it so important to impress his guardian with his dedication. He did not know how Dulitski earned his living, but from hints dropped by both Dulitski and other adults at the kibbutz he knew that his uncle was somehow involved with the politics of the country. Instinct told David that he was connected with the intelligence service. There was no reason to suppose he was not. The security which seemed to surround Dulitski's movements made it more, rather than less, likely. If he had held a straightforward government job there would be no reason for any security at all. David had few heroes in his life; the memory of his parents, and a pride in what they had done and how they had died was very important to him, but his guardian was a reality, a person he could know, love and revere. At this stage in his life, his loyalty to his country was perhaps partly due to the romanticism of youth – but only partly.

Dulitski had watched David develop and was daily becoming more sure of him.

Chapter 3

David could not know quite how important Dulitski was, nor how interested his uncle – and others – were in his future.

After the seriousness and the joyful celebration of the Bar Mitzvah, life returned to normal for him and his friends. At school, David continued to work hard; his exercise books were neat and his homework conscientiously done. 'Outstanding' was a frequent comment in his school reports. By taste and aptitude, mathematics and languages were his best subjects and he excelled in them both. He was also a born athlete and often went swimming in the Sea of Galilee. Afterwards he would go for long runs along the lakeside, easily outpacing other friends who occasionally joined him. David was always full of ideas. He invented games and made up long, complex fairy stories to keep the younger children at the kibbutz amused. But because he was without any superficial vanity he never aroused jealousy among his peers despite his achievements. He was kind and generous-hearted and as willing to join in the odd escapade as the rest of the boys. Dulitski, from a distance, noticed everything and approved.

When David was eighteen, he left school and was called up for National Service. By now, it was generally accepted that David's military service would lead to greater things. His real aim, although he told no one but Dulitski, was to enter the Mossad, the branch of the Israeli Secret Service which operates in the shadows overseas. It is perhaps one of the world's smaller intelligence services, but is regarded as one of the best. David's problem was that Mossad, like the other intelligence services of Israel, follows a strict policy of not accepting volunteers for field work. Dulitski had told David firmly, 'Israel doesn't want any desperadoes. It's up to you to prove yourself, work hard.'

Dulitski's warning had been unnecessary. David knew that his training would demand extremes of both physical and mental endurance. He had to go through his three years of military service. He also knew that from the day he began he would be constantly watched and reported on by everyone around him.

During his last six months of service David was assigned to Shyettet 13, the notoriously tough sea commandos. Day after day David's body and mind were stretched to the ultimate; every morning he would wake thinking he could not go on, but every evening he would fall heavily and dreamlessly asleep, having been pushed one step further than the day before. After the first month, he became accustomed to this constant pressure and began to marvel at what he and his instructors had achieved.

David knew that every time he pushed himself it was for his country. His body broadened and hardened until it was no longer recognisable as that of the lanky youth who had started his national service three years earlier.

A few days before the passing out ceremony David went for his usual run along the beach. He had not gone far when he was aware of someone behind him. The stranger called his name and, smiling, asked if he would care for a stroll along the beach. David, intrigued, said that he would. As they walked the stranger told him that the Mossad had taken a serious interest in him since he had begun military service and that it was the Mossad itself that had placed him in Shyettel 13. The man then introduced himself as Avi Lerner, a high-ranking intelligence officer in the Mossad.

'If you are interested in a future with us,' he continued, 'we are ready to consider your application as a recruit.' David was so surprised that for a moment he was speechless, then, overcoming a tremendous urge to jump in the air and shout with triumph, he replied with a broad grin, 'Where do I sign?'

In the following weeks David saw a lot of Avi Lerner. They met daily and had long discussions on a broad range of subjects – the agent had to be sure that David's reasons for joining the Mossad were the right ones. Avi took his time, knowing how vital it was to understand the mentality of the men you employed for dangerous field work. The Mossad required its members to obey orders without question, to be part of a dedicated team and yet at the same time to be a daring loner; the amalgam was rare and difficult to define, but Avi was trained to recognise it. One month after leaving the Army, Avi Lerner visited David at the kibbutz. 'As far as I'm concerned,' he said, 'you're in, but now you've got to convince the shrinks that you're up to the job.'

So David underwent a series of stringent medical and psychological tests. Men alone, in a hostile country with an assumed identity and without family or friends, suffer enormous stress. The tests were tough, but they were realistic. David had never experienced anything like it and hoped he never had to again. All the information gathered was fed into computers and analysed by teams of experts. The size of the Mossad is tiny next to that of the CIA or the KGB yet its range of activities are the same so it is essential that only the best are chosen. They take no chances.

Finally, David was told that he had been given a top

rating. 'You can join us – if you're still interested,' announced Avi, who was almost as delighted as David.

Avi explained the terms and rules for enlistment into the Secret Service. He would receive full salary from the first day of training. He would, like all other recruits, undergo an intensive six-month training course, in the practical and theoretical techniques of espionage. 'At the end of the training period you may leave or stay,' Avi explained. 'In fact that remains true during your entire career with us. Spies are like cooks,' he added, 'impossible to employ unless their heart is in it. The one condition we do insist upon – and I must make this very clear,' he added, 'is that you may never tell a single soul the true nature of your work – not even your wife, should you marry. Disregard of this one condition will mean instant dismissal.'

David gave his pledge of secrecy and told his friends and the kibbutz that he had landed a job with the Department of Trade. To Dulitski he said the same thing. Years later he would always remember that moment as the one when he stepped out of the real world and into the secret one.

David began his training in a three-room apartment in Tel Aviv which he shared with Avi Lerner. It was rented by the Mossad for just that purpose and there he stayed for the entire six months, studying the Mossad curriculum. He was not allowed to leave without permission and never unaccompanied. In the course of David's training, a special bond grew up between him and Avi. This was not only a deep friendship but also a tactical necessity. Senior officials knew that an agent living a lonely and dangerous life in a strange country needs to trust the links with the head office.

At the end of the six months of isolation, David had all the theoretical and wherever possible the practical skills a spy could need: armed and unarmed combat, explosives and explosions, how to gather and analyse information and how to pick any kind of lock or safe as speedily as any first-class burglar. And above all he had learned the need to be totally alert. To miss or forget anything, even something as seemingly trivial as whether he had closed the door behind him, was a cardinal sin in the eyes of his instructors.

There was one more important test David had to pass before qualifying for field work. He went on to the streets of Tel Aviv, followed by fellow recruits. He must first identify his trackers, then give them the slip without changing his behaviour pattern – a very difficult skill to master but one which one day might save his life. For a whole week he left the house in the morning and spent the day evading the 'shadows', and each day his performance improved. At first, he imagined he was being followed when he was not, and was often closely followed when he thought he was safe. But by the end of the week he could spot a shadow within seconds and lose him within minutes.

In the second week positions were reversed. David became the tracker while the others tried to give him the slip. David greatly enjoyed this part of his training. He also discovered he had a wild sixth sense, of supreme value to an agent in the mad illogical world of espionage and terrorism.

On the last day of the training period Avi and David were sitting drinking coffee in the tiny flat which David hoped never again to see.

'Well, how does it feel to be one of the family?' asked Avi.

'It's the only family I've ever had,' David replied.

Six weeks later David was given his first mission. It was

not a big job in itself but the Mossad does not waste its manpower and so his small effort was an important piece of a large and complex whole. He was to go to Berlin, posing as a businessman, and to follow the movements of an Arab leader over a couple of weeks.

On his return Dulitski asked David to come and see him.

'Well, David?' he smiled at his favourite.

'I must admit my main feeling is ambition,' David said. 'In fact, I've set my sights on the chair you're sitting in,' he added with a grin.

'Good. Let your ambition encourage you but don't let it take over from your good sense.' Dulitski's often expressionless face melted into a smile of real warmth and love.

It hadn't taken David long to discover that his uncle was the head of Israel's intelligence service – the *memuneh*. For over five years he had controlled intelligence operations virtually single-handed. Answering only to the Prime Minister, he was effectively the second most powerful man in Israel.

'Your mother – your parents – would have been proud of you.' Dulitski, who always looked people straight in the eyes, shuffled some papers on his desk.

'Yes?' David was puzzled.

'I was in love with your mother.'

'What?'

'We met in Trieste in 1938 and became close friends on the boat journey to Jaffa. Before long I joined the Haganah and because of our friendship Ruth became interested and helped us by carrying weapons – we knew the British rarely searched women.'

'Yes.' David knew this part of the story. That Dulitski had been in love with his mother was a revelation to him, but it helped explain many things.

86

'Your mother was a very courageous woman, but I've always felt partly to blame for what happened.'

'But so many people died in the kibbutz.'

Dulitski ignored him. 'While fighting with the Jewish underground I was promoted to an intelligence unit. I took Ruth with me. Soon after the Second World War she was posted to set up a new cell abroad – that was how she met your father. She was a lovely girl, so hopeful and dedicated . . .'

'Was she in love with you?'

'No. I'd always known I was in love with her, but knew I'd spoil it by telling her. She didn't feel the same way about me – that was my tragedy. I've never known anyone like her. I just wanted to tell you that: how much I loved her, and how proud I am of you.'

Every time Dulitski spoke of his mother, David's pride in her increased. He sometimes wondered why so little was said about his father, but Dulitski's confession explained this silence. As David had so often asserted, his lack of a real family made his dedication to Israel the stronger.

But at the same time he passionately wanted to live up to his parents and to be worthy of their memory. He wanted Dulitski to look at him and think 'that boy has something of Ruth in him. She would have been proud'.

Ruth would indeed have been proud. No one apart from some of the other Mossad agents had any idea that David was part of one of the most effective intelligence organisations in the world. He worked in France, England, North and South America and several Arab countries, and his natural ear as well as his training made him quickly fluent in several languages. Gradually, he became entrusted with more and more important jobs, and it was not only Dulitski who held the young man in high esteem for his loyalty, intelligence and the unfailingly high quality of his work.

Twice during his career in the Mossad David was called upon to assassinate. The first time was in the early seventies when a fresh campaign of terrorism was launched by various Palestinian organisations against the State of Israel. What made this new campaign different from previous action was that for the first time the Palestinians were practising their terrorism in Europe and on a scale calculated to attract maximum publicity and carnage. The Mossad ordered reports from its field agents and the picture that emerged from the amassed dossiers was one of organised terrorism on such a vast scale that it horrified the Mossad and her Western counterparts. Hardly a city in Europe was without its cell of Palestinians and its networks were linked with other bizarre terrorist groups. The Israelis had established that the Palestinians had linked up with the Provisional IRA, the Baader-Meinhof group and the Italian Red Brigade, among many others. Even more disturbing to Israel and her allied intelligence services was evidence that Black September, the terrorist arm of the PLO, was backed and often directed by the KGB. While Europe's governments dithered, the Mossad acted swiftly. Their crack agents were sent out to hunt down and liquidate the terrorist bosses wherever they were. If they could wipe out the top men they would seriously undermine the structure of the terrorist network.

In September 1972 David was posted to Paris to track down and eliminate Wadal Adel Zvaiter, a Palestinian who (beside writing poetry) masterminded the planting of bombs on aircraft and was behind the Munich Olympic Games Massacre. Three weeks later, on October 16th, David shot him dead.

The second time David killed a man was altogether

more disturbing. Agents in Paris had informed headquarters that they had a sighting of Machmud Assiz, top man on Israel's hit list. The Mossad had been hunting him for years as he had managed to keep his movements secret. Several previous attempts to scrub him out were aborted; he had always succeeded in giving them the slip. This time they were not going to take any chances. David had orders to shoot the man on sight.

Machmud Assiz was hidden out in rooms rented in the name of his younger brother, Hamdi. The owner of the house was an Algerian woman who occupied the ground floor apartment. David could see the woman, small and dark, watching television. David waited until nightfall, then dismissed the watchers and Rosenthal, the recognition expert. Assured that his target was safely housed, David had no more need of them. One last time he went over the layout of the house in his mind and then crossed the street and rang the bell of Assiz's landlady.

Madame de Tensenten opened the door to a tall, handsome and very correct looking Frenchman, smiling warmly.

David said languidly, '*Bonsoir, Madame. Je suis venu voir Monsieur Assiz. Je m'excuse de vous avoir dérangée.*' Beneath his exterior calm his heart was controlled but beating fast. His mind was ice-cold.

The woman was charmed. '*Je vous en prie.*'

She let him in and, with a practised smile of thanks, David crossed the hall to the far door which he knew led to the narrow flight of stairs to Assiz's room. The adrenalin was pumping into his veins now, the sound of his own footsteps echoing in his own ears.

He was going to kill a man. His movements became automatic; his purpose cold and hard. He was a machine programmed by love for Israel. A vow made at a hot, dusty Bar Mitzvah had led him to this stairway in Paris.

Behind him, Madame de Tensenten was urging him to take off his coat, but her voice was a distant backdrop. He ran lightly up the stairs, hands going for the automatic pistol in his shoulder holster. Fluid, practised, gun out, silencer from its leather pouch; in, one turn, two, three, final twist, silencer in place, slide back, hammer cocked, two hands on the pistol grip.

Then the door, a murmur of conversation behind it, his foot up to waist height, a kick, the door splintering open.

There in a tableau was Machmud Assiz looking up from a small table piled high with books and papers, bent in the classic scholar's manner, his face showing first surprise, then fear. And another figure in the photographic image that would never leave David's mind. A youth, sitting on the narrow bed. His mouth opened to scream.

David crouched, automatic levelled, arms bent at the elbow, body behind the weapon, foresight and backsight lined up. Assiz was frozen in shock.

The boy screamed.

David fired once, twice, two heavy, ugly plop-plopping sounds from the silenced gun, and Assiz was lifted and slammed back against the wall, body arching, a spray of blood splattering the paintwork. David turned, lined the gun on the boy. For an instant only. The boy was not the target.

Then David was out of the room, down the stairs, unscrewing the silencer, stowing it and the automatic into the shoulder holster, brushing past the bewildered, terrified woman in the hall, and out into the street.

Within five minutes David was in a different *arrondissement* and his heartbeat was normal.

Three days later he was back at the headquarters in Tel Aviv.

Lerner said bluntly, and without preamble: 'I'm afraid

90

there was a mistake on your last job.'

David stiffened in his chair. This was his living nightmare, the thing he had most dreaded.

'What kind of mistake?'

'Rosenberg identified the wrong man.'

'My God!' David gripped the arms of the chair until his knuckles were bloodless. Rosenberg was the 'bumps' man, the recognition expert, the one who had given the go-ahead once he had identified the target.

'Who was it?' David said coldly, his voice cracking.

'Does it matter?'

'Who *was* it?'

'*Hamdi* Assiz, the target's brother. He was an academic trying to get a teaching job in Paris.'

'Political connections? Was he with Black September, PLO, anyone?'

'None, I'm afraid. He kept clear of politics. David, I am bitterly sorry. Rosenberg has been disciplined.'

Lerner felt David was taking it badly. If there could be such a thing as a moral killer, then perhaps David and those in the Mossad were that paradox.

'I should have checked him myself, dammit,' David said, clenching his fists in anger, 'Damn Rosenberg. *Damn* him!'

'You are trained to kill Israel's enemies, my friend, you are unlike other men.'

'I killed an innocent man.'

'You did your job! And if every Mossad agent checked every order before it was carried out Israel would have long since perished. What happened was regrettable.'

'Regrettable! I blew out the brains of an innocent man and it is merely *regrettable?* What are we in the Mossad? Thugs, Mafiosi? His face . . . oh God, I'll never forget that face as long as I live. He died not even understanding why.'

Lerner put his hand on David's shoulder. He could see the fire in David's eyes. 'Look, I am sorry, Rosenberg is sorry, we are *all* sorry. But there is nothing we can do. The Mossad is not infallible. We can only learn from this and see it does not happen again.'

David stood up and Lerner's hand fell from his shoulder: 'Of course. But I hope you'll excuse me, I feel an urgent need to get drunk.' He saw the look of alarm in Lerner's eyes. Drink. Talk. Security. They'd hold David by force if necessary. 'Don't look so worried, my friend, I am still Mossad. I shall stay in my apartment, the telephone will be off the hook, I shall talk to no one. But if anyone tries to stop me leaving the building, I'll kick the shit out of him.'

Lerner let him go.

But the incident made a deeper impression than Lerner realised at the time. It almost cost David his nerve. He went on working and his performance was of as high a standard as ever. But he began to brood. He was then thirty-three. The age for retirement in the Mossad is thirty-six. After that, ex-agents are used for consultation or training. David began to look forward to retirement from active service and even to hope that he might be allowed to retire early. He had put in a good stint. He was not disillusioned with the Mossad and believed as strongly as ever in Israel and her fight for survival; but he was disillusioned with himself. He even began to wish that in his wanderings he had found himself a wife. He had never had a family, so perhaps he felt the lack of one less than other men might, but now he wondered at his life. All his emotion had been spent on his work and his love of his country. He had had many affairs, some in the line of business and some purely for pleasure, but he had never really known love.

In the end he did not take early retirement. By the time

he had started to consider it he had only a year more anyway, and decided he might as well go on until the end.

Nevertheless he was taken aback by Dulitski's latest order. He knew it was the most important job he had ever been given and that if he succeeded he would be regarded as one of the heroes of the Mossad. He knew he should be proud to have been chosen. He *was* proud, but something in Dulitski's manner made him wish he could back out and let the opportunity pass. Yet, the whole story was so fantastic, so frightening in its implications, that it must be true. There was no doubt the man must be killed. Somehow David felt that he was the man to do it.

PART THREE

WASHINGTON

Chapter 1

Amethyst slammed the car door and drove towards Georgetown. Today she had probably done one of the worst celebrity interviews of her career. Alley Cat, the super-sexy American recording star, had been hers for the questioning and Amethyst had turned up hoping to catch sight of the woman behind the image. What had made Alison Katz into Alley Cat, the foul-mouthed, pouting sex kitten of the eighties? From the moment she had entered the room, Amethyst had sensed trouble. It was called giving a reporter a bad time. Alley Cat the public image was all there was, a beautiful, empty box, probably very rich by now. Sex kitten? 'More like a bloody pedigree bitch,' Amethyst muttered to herself as she swung the car into the gravel drive. She would just have to pad the article out somehow.

She parked the car and gave the Corvette's bonnet an affectionate pat as she walked round it. Henry had given it to her to make up for having to leave her Porsche behind in London. She knew she was spoilt, but quite frankly she loved it. She was new enough to this extravagant way of life still to take a childish pleasure in the toys that were part of the package, but sophisticated enough to treat everything as though she were to the manner born.

Best among the 'toys' was the beautiful house in the smart suburb of Washington. There was something almost, but not quite, English about it which had made her feel instantly at home. Set back from the road and with a pleasant garden, the house was one in a street of imposing mansions. The sycamore trees lining the road and the gravel sweeps in front of the houses seemed to be aiming at an American conception of Old World elegance.

Amethyst grinned to herself as she ran lightly up the broad steps to the front door. How silly to worry about one article when her life was otherwise in such good order. Buster opened the door to her with his usual wide smile.

'Afternoon, Missy. Have you had a good day?'

'Thank you, Buster, not too bad. Is Mr Brauner back yet?'

Buster came especially high on her list of the real prizes in her new life. He was terrifyingly like Oddjob until he smiled, which he did most of the time – 'Smiles like he's running for Mayor', as Sylvia had once commented. He had been Henry's valet for years and was now elevated to butler. At first he had regarded Amethyst with polite suspicion. After several days she had concluded that he was merely checking her over, rather like a new pair of shoes, to see if she was up to his master's standards. Somewhere along the line she had gained his approval and they were now firm friends.

'Still out, Missy. But he'll be back well in time for dinner.'

'Oh God – dinner! I'd better go and have a word with Sarah.'

She crossed the high-ceilinged hall, grateful for the cool of the marble and air-conditioning after the stifling heat of a Washington October afternoon. She went into a neatly organised office.

'Sarah, be an angel and fill me in on tonight's guest list. Henry did run through it with me but I'd like to check it over with you.'

Sarah Cohen looked up irritably from her typewriter, but she quickly gave way to a smile. Few could resist Amethyst for long and by now the whole of Brauner's staff had grown to like her – even Kelly was beginning to thaw. Sarah was Brauner's small, plump and very Jewish appointments secretary. Unmarried and in her late thirties, people said of her that she had fallen into the age-old secretary's syndrome and was in love with Henry. If so, she never let it show in her relations with either Brauner or Amethyst.

'Sure thing,' she said, running a finger down a list to her left. 'We've got Lee Iacocca – the Chrysler man – and his wife Mary.' She looked up. 'He's so popular around here it's said he could be elected to any office he wanted, for life. They're meant to be great company – you should like them. Then we have Frank and Geraldine O'Connor. Not very important yet but Frank is rising fast and could be useful. She's well known to be fun.'

'He's a politician?'

'Yep, and she was an actress. Former good-time girl who is not really sure what's hit her but is learning fast. She's got bright red hair and the most awesome mammaries. Once the guys on the Hill lost interest in whether or not Reagan dyed his hair, the next big question was whether or not Geraldine had had implants. Henry took her out a few times – pre A.B. days, of course,' she added with a smile.

Henry was as reticent about the women in his past as he was about everything else. Amethyst knew of his reputation as one of Washington's leading swingers, but he himself was silent on the subject and would not be teased into saying anything. On the few occasions when she had questioned him about one of his more publicised affairs he had avoided giving any direct reply. Perhaps it

99

was an old-fashioned sense of gallantry, but Amethyst thought it was more likely to be his usual passion for secrecy.

'Sounds like my kind of girl. OK. Who else?'

'Joe Betleheim – he's a top surgeon and charges that way.'

'I know his name. He's not the man who operated on the world's most publicised colon a while back?'

'Let's say you're on the right track. He's very popular and his passion is collecting modern American paintings, so he should hit it off well with the Carolettis. They are down from New York preparing for the opening of their new gallery next month.' Amethyst liked Jack and Ann Caroletti; they genuinely loved art and were very knowledgeable. She herself was becoming interested in buying pictures and hoped to pick up a few tips.

'The numbers seem to be uneven.'

'Oh yes – Mrs Benson's coming.'

'Sylvia! How stupid of me to forget. I haven't seen her for a few weeks. I'd better book her for a lunch as we won't be able to have a real gas tonight.'

'Gas?' Sarah was politely puzzled.

'What? Oh, you know; natter, chat, jaw, *gossip*, Sarah. We're meant to speak the same language.'

'I know, and it's called English, not American – I'll say so before you do.' The two women laughed: whenever the 'language problem' came up they sparred patriotically.

'OK, you win. I'd better pop in and see Bertha. Thanks for the rundown.' Amethyst picked up her tape recorder and notebooks from Sarah's desk and went back into the hall. Leaving her things on the console table at the bottom of the stairs so that she would remember to take them upstairs with her, she went into the shadowy far end of the hall and, turning right, swung open the silent green baize door and went through to the domestic staff quarters.

The kitchen was a fine example of beautiful craftsmanship. It combined an air of a traditional kitchen with every imaginable mechanical device. A huge marble pastry table was set against one wall and the shelves gleamed with the rows of glass and metal mixers, cutters, shakers and stirrers. It was a kitchen any woman would love to be in control of and Amethyst wished she could occasionally do some cooking there, but every person in Brauner's household had his or her allotted place; Amethyst was the writer, not the cook.

'Afternoon, Miss Amethyst. You gettin' ready fo' tonight?' Bertha turned from supervising a nervous teenager's attempt to work the vegetable slicer. Bertha was fat and black, and a relatively new member of Brauner's entourage; Sylvia had found her while staying with friends near Savannah. She had immediately rung Brauner, informed him he needed a new cook, asked him if he was prepared to pay very well and poached Bertha from her friends, who had taken some time to forgive her. Brauner on the other hand was suitably grateful, and Bertha was very happy in her new home. Amethyst wanted Bertha and Buster to marry 'like they do in books', but neither Bertha nor Buster seemed to share her wish.

'Hi, Bertha. I'm on my way up but thought I'd pay you a visit and see what's cooking. All set?'

'Sure am. Lovage soup, duck breasts on spinach with a madeira and *foie gras* sauce, cheese and raspberry pavlova. That suit you?'

'Sounds wonderful. Bertha, you're a dream. I won't be able to eat for a week afterwards.'

'One thing about you, Miss Amethyst, is you're a girl who can eat. None of this namby-pamby pokin' and pickin' at yo' food. It's a pleasure to cook fo' you.'

'Well, thank you,' Amethyst laughed. 'You're right, although I've no doubt retribution will come. Anyway I'd better go up and relax before dressing for dinner.'

Back in the hall she saw that her things had been moved from where she left them. She was still not used to being waited on. At first she had assumed that she had mislaid her possessions, but gradually she had come to realise that unseen hands, like Baden-Powell's Brownies, cleared up behind her almost before she had left a room.

She ran up the wide stairs, her eyes drawn as always to the early American art which lined the walls. At the top she turned left and paused a moment from habit outside Henry's rooms, then reached her own door. She and Brauner had separate suites at opposite ends of the first-floor landing. Most people knew that Amethyst and Brauner were lovers, but Washington still demanded that conventions be observed. Although unofficially regarded as mistress of the house, officially she was a guest or even a privileged member of the staff, higher than the rest, but not a member of the family. Somewhat along the lines of a Victorian governess, she often thought.

Amethyst herself was not at all sure of the exact nature of their relationship. Late one night when they were in bed Henry had surprised her.

'I think we ought to make plans,' he had said.

'I thought you were asleep.'

'I don't sleep much.' If at all, Amethyst thought. After making love he would lie very still and close his eyes but she often doubted that he was asleep. Usually when she woke, his side of the bed was empty and she found him dressed or on the telephone.

He switched on the light next to him and looked at her.

'What sort of plans?' she said.

He hesitated. 'About the future.'

'Henry, are you proposing marriage?'

'Yes, I think I am,' he said, sounding almost as surprised as she felt. 'I love you.'

She kissed him. 'I should hope so, but do you trust me?'

He laughed. 'Love and trust at my age are a risky business.'

'You're not old.'

'I'm old enough to be wary of being foolish. I don't like admitting it, but I do need you – and I've never said that to anyone before.' He paused for a moment. 'I've always felt it a weakness.'

As she hesitated he added, on a lighter note, 'I shall propose to you officially in a rather more dignified position.' He had not mentioned it again.

Amethyst knew as much as a woman could know that he had been sincere and she had spent a lot of time thinking it over. She was thinking about it now as she crossed the room to her wardrobe. There was no question that her life would be one of hard work and material ease. She liked most of his friends; she had learned to cope with the publicity aspect, and even to enjoy it. She believed Henry loved her as much as he had ever loved anyone. She was not so sure about herself. She loved his company, and they were sexually and mentally totally attuned – but she just was not sure. She was unable to come to a decision one way or the other. Still, why rush? There was all the time in the world.

She smiled as she slipped out of her grey linen suit and wrapped herself in a white kimono. She bent and picked up her clothes and put them on the chaise longue at the end of the large bed. What she needed now was a hot shower and then a stiff drink. She wished Henry were back. Before going through into the bathroom she lifted the internal telephone and dialled.

'Sarah? Do you know where Henry is?'

'He went to play chess with Senator Sharp'.

Senator Ben Sharp was captain of the ship most likely to steam into the White House. He was also the richest man in the United States Senate. 'Too rich to be bribed, too intelligent to be compromised.' he had once boomed at Amethyst and she had believed him. They liked each other, which was just as well as Henry and the Senator spent a lot of time together. Henry briefed him on foreign policy issues, and was his director in a series of foreign policy studies. They also shared a common passion for tennis and chess.

'Said he'd be back by seven.'

Amethyst looked at her watch. It was a small Cartier wristwatch dating from the nineteen-twenties. Originally designed for French tank commanders during the First World War, it was one of the few mementoes she had of her father's family – it had been his mother's and he had given it to her on the last birthday before he died. It was now a quarter to six, and Cartier were never wrong.

'Well, if you see him before you go, tell him I'm in the music room. I'm going to take a shower, then move on up there.'

'OK. Have a great party.'

The bathroom was spectacular: the bath stood on four lion's feet in the middle of the room and the shower was set in the mahogany panelling which lined the room. Brass gleamed and marble shone in the mirrored glass ceiling. Most luxurious of all, there was a large fireplace.

Amethyst took her shower as hot as her skin could bear it, and then turned the cold full on. Stepping out, she wrapped a large pale-blue robe around her and swathed a matching towel turban-like over her dripping hair. She dried herself and went up a floor to the music room.

The music room was not entirely appropriately named; as well as containing the music system and the television, it was also the home for every kind of electronic toy. Brauner delighted in such things and was constantly buying the latest gadget as it appeared on the market.

Opening a Queen Anne chest which contained a drinks cabinet, Amethyst poured herself a gin and tonic and walked slowly over to the ceiling-high bookshelf which was filled with books on Brauner's special interest, twentieth century military history. Once again she noticed with pride that Henry read in at least five languages. Amethyst liked this room best of all and it was the only one in which she felt really at home. Although there was a small sitting room on the ground floor reserved for her use, she spent as much time as she could in the music room. Sipping at her drink, she put some jazz on the turntable and with it playing quietly in the background, curled up on the sofa and picked up the latest copy of *Vogue*. She had plenty of time before she need start getting ready. Half reading, half daydreaming, she passed about half an hour before the door flew open and Brauner burst in with much more than his usual exuberance.

'Buster's bringing up some champagne,' he said, and paused to admire her for a moment.

'Champagne? I'm sorry, I was half asleep. What's the celebration?'

'Come here.' He pulled her off the sofa and kissed her warmly. There was a discreet cough at the door and Buster appeared grinning widely and carrying a silver tray with ice bucket and champagne. Dressed for the dinner party, he looked positively festive with his white gloves and starched collar. Putting the tray on a side table he left the room quietly.

'What's he so happy about?' laughed Brauner, pulling Amethyst to him and slipping a hand inside her robe.

105

'What are *you* so happy about? I know – you've just checkmated Bobby Fischer,' she teased.

Brauner looked at Amethyst for a moment, and she noticed a curious gleam in his blue eyes that was at once triumphant and remote.

'Even better,' he said, brightening. 'Ben just asked me to start thinking how I would reorganise the State Department. Of course,' he added quickly, 'it doesn't mean a thing until he's in the Oval Office, but it's great for starters.'

'Henry! How wonderful. Where's that champagne?'

Brauner let go of her, opened the bottle with a deft twist and poured some champagne into two glasses from the chest. He handed Amethyst one and sank into the sofa. She sat beside him and, leaning close against him, drank some of the fizzy liquid.

'Pink champagne! Here's to a rosy future.' They raised their glasses high and with mock seriousness toasted each other.

'And if it is to be Henry Brauner, Secretary of State, will Amethyst Brauner be standing beside him as he starts his tenure?'

She hesitated for a moment. 'If we get in,' she smiled at the plural, 'I shall consider it my patriotic duty to marry you. At least I won't have to change my initials. But,' she added quickly, 'let's set our sights on the White House first.'

'Yep. It's a ripe moment for us old hard-liners. Ben wants foreign policy to be one of our major campaign issues.'

Amethyst tipped her head back and looked up at him. She liked it when he talked openly to her like this. It was all too rare and she appreciated it. She knew from past experience that he did not like to be questioned. And

106

there was also the security angle. He needed to be led most gently.

'What happens next?'

'Next, my angel, I'm going to whisk you off to Harold's place at the Keys.'

'Will Harold and Mary be there?'

'Sure, and they're expecting us. We'll go for a long weekend, take a real break and come back ready for the attack.'

'You know something, Henry?' Amethyst spoke hesitantly, knowing how much he disliked such avowals, 'I'm happy, really happy.'

'Me too.' He chuckled lightly and, tightening his arm around her, kissed her again. She returned his kisses and, turning, burrowed her head into his chest. A hand stroked her neck and hair while the other slipped back under the robe.

'No work this weekend,' he murmured in a low voice. 'I promise.'

'My sentiments exactly.' She looked up at him mischievously but as their eyes met her expression softened and he felt her body lean against his. She put her chin up and he bent to kiss her again, this time with a force that left no doubt as to what he wanted.

They were ready for dinner only minutes before the first guests arrived.

The following afternoon Amethyst and Brauner boarded Harold Jay's white Gulfstream 3 which had been sent up to Washington for them. Amethyst had protested mildly, saying they could easily catch a commercial flight, but Harold had dismissed the suggestion.

'Now listen, honey, what is the point of the goddamn thing just sitting down here getting a suntan? If I need her

I'd tell you straight out. She could use a run anyway. You're cleared for take-off at four pm. That suit you?'

'That would be lovely. See you in time for dinner.'

The Flying Pig was a beautiful object, fitted out in red and black lacquer, brass and tan pigskin (hence her nickname). She seated six passengers in total comfort and could fly just about anywhere in the world. Harold had a quick turnover of staff – something Amethyst found symptomatic of an untrustworthy man – and a new beautiful girl was always at hand to serve a variety of drinks. Although by now Amethyst was quite at ease in Harold's company, there was still something about him she didn't quite like although she could not put her finger on it. She secretly wished that the Jays were not going to be at the Keys that weekend. But Harold was right in thinking that his jet would be considerably more comfortable than a commercial flight and the way the airline news had been going lately she was a lot less likely to fall out of the sky.

Amethyst settled back in one of the leather armchairs with a rug drawn up over her knees while Henry switched on the lacquer and brass console which housed a communications system, and glanced at the New York Stock Exchange figures. He was in a rare mood of relaxation.

'Henry, you promised!' Amethyst teased.

Brauner switched off and took her hand, giving it a small apologetic squeeze. 'Force of habit,' he said, laughing at himself. 'For the next few days you will have my undivided attention.'

Jay's driver was waiting for them on the tarmac at Miami Airport and the luggage was quickly and efficiently transferred to the Mercedes limousine – one of Amethyst's favourite perks of high living. Soon the car was speeding down the US 1. Amethyst loved this part of the journey.

For her, the names of the various Keys always evoked Humphrey Bogart and Sidney Greenstreet: Key Largo, Tavanier, Plantation Creek.

It was not long before the big car swung through the large black iron gates into the grounds of Coral Creek. The sun was just setting as the car emerged from the shadow of a jungle of coco palms and drew to a halt in front of the main house. For a man of Jay's wealth it wasn't showy. It sprawled lazily, Southern fashion, and Harold had made liberal use of railroad sleepers, native key stone and bleached pine. What made it really spectacular was the setting. Jay had imported a desert island atmosphere, with the white sandy beach and the royal palms regally grouped around the house and pool. But the coral sea and the wide blue skies were there by divine will.

Within minutes Mary was welcoming them warmly and Harold effusively.

'Hi there, you guys, had a good flight? Ammy, you look great as always,' Amethyst checked her irritation at the abbreviation of her name and held out her cheek to be kissed. 'You're in the guest cottage as usual,' he continued. 'You know the way. I'm just about to mix up some poppers or would you prefer anything else?' Poppers were Harold's latest drink fad – two parts tequila to one part Seven Up were banged sharply in the glass until the liquid turned to bubbles. You drank it down in one gulp and got an implosion as the bubbles hit your stomach and reverted to liquid. 'Poppers for you both? Great. They'll be ready.'

'He's taken to bullying me almost as badly as he does Mary,' Amethyst commented as Arthur the driver placed the Vuitton bags and Henry's briefcase in the bedroom. 'Even if it is only to make me comfortable.'

'Will that be all, ma'am?'

'Yes, Arthur, thank you. Good night.'

It was good to be back. Amethyst kicked off the uncomfortable high-heeled shoes and looked around her. Her eyes swept over the large carved bed, canopied in white muslin, the bleached hardwood floors and the wide pastel rugs. Taking a hairbrush, she walked slowly to the living room which had a high-beamed ceiling adorned with circular fans to keep it cool. A large picture window in one of the simple stucco walls overlooked the water. The place always gave her a sense of ease and peace: a much-needed calm after the frantic pace of Washington.

'You're looking ridiculously like a mermaid right now,' said Henry, turning towards her, laughing. 'Brushing out your blonde curls. Why don't you sing, and bully Harold right back?'

'I'll drink my popper and flutter my eyelashes instead. Are you ready? Let's go.'

Dinner was fun. Harold had lit the barbecue, enjoying his role as the great outdoors man. Amethyst always liked the Jays more on their Keys territory than anywhere else. Mary was more forthcoming and Harold less overbearing than usual. After dinner Henry went off for a jacuzzi and a late swim while Amethyst sat with Harold on the terrace drinking coffee and chatting idly.

'What do you make of Ben Sharp's comment to Henry?' Amethyst asked, watching Brauner stopping to talk to one of the groundsmen who was doing a late night check around the estate.

Amethyst had always liked and trusted Ben Sharp, not only as one of Henry's few real friends, but politically. Sylvia had introduced Henry and Ben early on in Henry's political climb, and Amethyst knew that Sylvia's judgement of people was generally right. She later found out that Jay had engineered the meeting, which had slightly

110

dampened her enthusiasm until she had tackled Sylvia on the subject.

'Why sure, honey, Harold suggested it.' Sylvia had looked surprised. 'But how do you think I ever met Henry? I'd known Harold for years, long before Henry came along, although I'd heard a lot about him from Harold. As soon as we met I knew he was just what the Republicans needed. And then Harold said to me, "Now listen here, Sylvie, what's the point of you keeping these two boys apart?"' Amethyst laughed as the shrill-voiced Sylvia tried in vain to impersonate Harold's low bellow. ' "Here's Henry, all set to break into politics," ' Sylvia continued, giving up her attempt at mimicry, ' "and there's Ben Sharp, who wines and dines you as many times a week as you want and is besotted with your every word." Of course, Harold didn't know what he was talking about. He's not very good at flattery,' Sylvia added, but Amethyst could see she preened herself on the idea of the powerful Senator's infatuation. 'But anyway by then I believed in Henry so I thought, why not? And as Harold said to me after the first meeting, "Sylvie, dear, I believe you've brought about an historic partnership." Mind you, I wasn't sure if he was going for flattery or pomposity at that stage.' They had been lunching at Sans Souci at the time; Sylvia's shriek of laughter had turned heads at neighbouring tables.

The result of this conversation was that Amethyst felt she could trust Ben, and she was sure that his hint about the reorganisation of the State Department had been carefully thought out in advance.

'I've no doubt it was a sincere offer – after all, Henry has offered advice to two Presidents,' said Harold. 'He's done a great job as the Director of the Institute of

111

Strategic Studies and I know Ben regards him as one of our most important "think tanks". Mind you, a lot of political juggling goes on before a cabinet is finally settled on.'

'Oh yes, I know that. Who is that man?' Amethyst's attention had been attracted by the man Brauner had been talking to earlier on.

'Who? Oh, that's Cundo. One of the groundsmen. He's from Cuba – been here for years. Why?'

'Well, apart from looming about looking like a stand-in for Arnold Schwarzenegger, he doesn't seem to do much . . . that's all,' she added lamely. Amethyst did not want to mention that she found the Cuban's attitude to his employer a shade too relaxed and that, frankly, he spooked her.

She watched him for a second longer and then turned back to Harold. Mary had gone into the house, and she was alone with her host. Harold's square open face had a sincere look about it and Amethyst decided it was a good opportunity to talk to him about Henry.

'Harold,' she started tentatively, 'you've known Henry better and for longer than anyone. I suppose he's told you that he's asked me to marry him?'

'If you're worrying whether he's got a mad wife in the attic, the answer's no,' said Harold, laughing.

'I didn't mean that,' said Amethyst with a grin. They were silent for a moment. 'Does he have any real family left?'

'Not that I know of – wiped out in a string of concentration camps.'

'He's never been too forthcoming about his past. He rarely talks of his family or his youth in Germany.'

'Too painful, I guess.' Jay's voice was wary in the darkness. 'He minimises the impact it must have had on his life – some kind of escapist therapy, I suppose.'

'Harold?' Mary's voice came from the lighted drawing-room window.

'She's right, we'd better go in.'

'I think I'll go to bed,' said Amethyst, stifling a yawn. 'Henry's been gone a while. I hope he hasn't been nabbed by the local Jaws. Perhaps he's gone straight back to the cottage. See you in the morning. Goodnight.'

As Amethyst walked across the lawn towards the guest house she thought about Brauner and felt a stab of pity. The war had always seemed so long ago. She must learn not to be too impatient with his silences or his evasions. She must learn to try to understand the terror of what he had lived through . . .

Had she known the truth, pity would have been the last thing in her heart.

PART FOUR

THE GROUNDWORK

Chapter 1

It was a sea of human flotsam, the debris of the biggest war in mankind's history: twenty thousand human beings speaking scores of languages and dialects, some without names, many without memory, all without a nation or a home they could now call their own.

In officialese it was called a Displaced Persons Camp, but the polite euphemism camouflaged the truth. These people were not displaced . . . they were uprooted, torn, dragged from everything they had ever known. Normality and reason had been swept from their lives by the hurricane of war and had come to rest in this place. And here they stayed, to contemplate the enormity of what had befallen them. Here was a polyglot mass of humanity stranded far from their homes, driven by fear, by force . . . the sheer terror and dislocation of war.

This vast compound now housed an enormous mongrel family in hastily-constructed wooden huts or olive-green tents, and out on the perimeter the biggest irony — a barbed-wire fence that ran around the camp, a bitter joke in a land that had turned itself into the biggest prison and torture chamber Europe had ever known. For the wire was to keep people out, not in. Inside was safety and security of sorts. Outside lay danger. Inside, these foreign soldiers — healthy, fit men from across the sea — fed the inhabitants, not tortured them; and gave them clothing and medical care.

It was to the gate of the Camp ZF23 that Alexander Trepov came, and there they took him in with the minimum

117

of questions and a kind of rough, military kindness. He was just one more hungry, pathetic face in a world that seemed full of nothing else.

And even he, with his hidden cunning and secret mission, was glad to be behind the barbed wire and the guns of the Americans. Outside, Germany was in the throes of a dying nightmare. Cities were laid to waste, a civilisation which had given Europe much before its decade of madness, was in ruins. To the East the new barbarians had come to revenge themselves for the obscenities their conquerors had inflicted upon their people. Behind the disciplined front-line troops came the rabble, a new Mongol horde who raped and killed at will. And it was from this world that Trepov walked with his historic destiny still so many years in the future.

The previous night he had taken refuge in a ditch. That morning he had woken to find he had been sleeping on a pile of corpses. The Germans had hardly taken trouble to shovel earth over them. Sickened and numb, he lay there, one foot on a thigh-bone. And then in the sheer panic of trying to claw his way out he had fallen back in again. He heard his nose break as bone hit bone and felt his mouth fill with blood, but it was only seconds before he was out of the ditch and running – running, as though the bodies were alive and vicious.

He would never be able to sleep like a child again.

At the edge of the forest, in terrible pain, he had crawled under a tree and made himself breathe in as deeply and as slowly as he could. These Germans were barbarians. 80 million, 80 million, people, he kept repeating to himself, had gone stark, staring and willingly mad. This wasn't the first time either, he thought to himself, that they had deserted civilisation for the bloodthirsty ethics of their Nordic gods.

118

His mother had been born a German Jewess, but like many Jewish intellectuals she had left for Russia in the late twenties, renouncing her nationality and religion. She had dreams of a world remade.

He had known (no, sensed, he corrected himself, hearing his instructor, Kruglor's, voice intoning, 'Knowledge comes from specifics'), that the next few months were going to be the most difficult part of the task. Suddenly, in spite of the pain, he felt hope again, and with all the dedication of youth and ideology he joined the weary mass of humanity that was already blocking the roads south and east of Berlin in a desperate search to find a British or American camp that would accept another starving family. Towards nightfall, he was in the American Zone. Half walking, half crawling, he reached the gates of an American Displaced Persons Camp and collapsed at the feet of the armed guards.

When Alexander came to, he was looking into the face of an aggressive-looking American with bright red hair cropped in military fashion.

'What's your name? Name, fahcrissake.'

As clearly as possible through a broken nose and in his most precise English he answered as he had been instructed.

'My name is Albrecht Junger.'

'Albrecht Junger?'

'Yes.' There was no hesitation.

'My name is Major Mitchell. Could you use some coffee?'

Coffee? He had never even seen coffee. He hesitated. It was a simple decision but the first outside his brief. For a second he looked forward apprehensively to the long life of deceit ahead of him. He had been told that in the years to come he would have to make many serious decisions. But this small matter of coffee brought home the fact to him.

119

'Yes, and could I have some sugar please?'

The major smiled, showing even pointed teeth like a prison guard dog. 'Now listen to me, Alby. I'm gonna ask you a few questions.' He was holding a large white card. 'Any family you know of?'

The boy lowered his head. 'Auschwitz, sir.'

This was all too depressingly familiar. 'How old are you?'

'Fifteen, sir.'

'Place of birth?'

'Berlin.'

'And how have you survived till now?'

Junger met the major's eye. 'In the forest, sir.'

Another forest refugee. The major sighed inwardly. How these kids had managed it he would never know.

Junger added a few details of the life of the dead boy whose place he had taken.

Jewish. Born, East Prussia. Mother, father, two brothers, one sister, deported to Auschwitz-Birkenau, April, 1943, all family exterminated. Boy put to work on Sonderkommandos, removing bodies from the gas chambers and taking them to the crematoria. Managed to escape west when SS started shooting Sonderkommandos on approach of Russian armies.

The story was too common to warrant any further interest. The Americans issued him with a food ration card and forgot him.

The camp was full to overflowing. When the Germans had surrendered, the Western Allies had over six million displaced persons in their area and on their hands. Junger kept much to himself during the following weeks, thinking hard of various ways to integrate himself with the Americans. The DPs were not popular with high-ranking officials who knew they had to live among the Germans for years to come and therefore sought to be conciliatory

120

towards them. The displaced persons, on the other hand, were a temporary nuisance and regarded as such.

The medical orderly who had patched up his nose presented the opportunity.

'How many languages do you speak, son?'

'Five, sir.'

'Five? Goddammit, five languages! Like what?'

'English, sir, I learn in school. German my tongue.'

'Yes, I know you're German and I can hear your English. What about the other three?'

'Russian, sir, many Russians in Auschwitz, Polish. Also one of the prisoners teach me a little French.'

'Go on, let's hear you.'

The man didn't know even one of the languages he was supposed to check, but he seemed satisfied when Junger rattled off what appeared to be some Russian, Polish and French.

'Some Czech also . . .'

'Whoa, hold your horses, five'll do fine. You're just what we need. We've got the whole of goddamn Europe out there. I can't understand a thing they're babbling at me. You can be my interpreter.' The boy looked blank. 'Interpreter? It means I tell you and you tell them. Then you tell me what they said back.'

'Yes, sir, I be your interpreter.'

'Right. You interpret. I'll dish out the medicine.'

Junger now had his own bunk and an armband that gave him access to all parts of the camp. The Americans were doing their best but the hygiene and medical care were well below what was needed – it was chaos and counter-chaos. Typhus was breaking out and the half-living shells, many still dressed in their prison stripes, were in desperate need of special food and medical aid.

Within a few months of Junger's arrival, the American Joint Distribution Company, fondly nicknamed 'The

121

Joint', had set up a separate camp for the Jews under the overall authority of the army. This was to take care of their special needs. Junger once again made himself useful, helping 'The Joint' set up schools.

One day, walking across the compound, he heard his name called in Russian. He almost faltered. His instinct was to run, but that was clearly impossible. So he kept on walking.

'Alex? Alexander Trepov?'

He felt a hand on his arm. Taking a deep breath he turned and looked up into a pair of familiar eyes. His heart began to beat violently. It was that goddamn Jew from the carpet shop in Moscow. With a tremendous effort, he forced himself to behave normally.

'I'm sorry,' he said, careful to accentuate the German guttural in the Russian. 'You must be mistaken. My name is Junger.' With perfect control he walked away as casually as possible but not before the Jew had looked straight at the boy's hand. Strange, he thought, I could have sworn it was the boy Alex. Tip of the finger missing too. But there was something different about the face. A pity – we could have played chess again. The Jew was tired and sick, half-starved. There were so many faces. So many faces you thought you knew. So perhaps it was not Trepov.

And yet the memory lodged there in his mind like a tiny grain that would one day grate and agitate until it reminded him.

Trepov in the camp. The boy with the missing fingertip. Or was it Junger? Perhaps Trepov just wanted to be Junger now. Everyone was paranoid in these awful days. A new name could mean a new face, old things forgotten, old crimes, perhaps, gone unpunished.

So Trepov was Junger, and Junger was Trepov. Maybe Trepov was dead and Junger was just Junger.

The Jew from the carpet shop repeated the words Trepov/Junger/Trepov/Junger like a litany as he trudged across the compound.

The world was crazy anyway. God could be called Junger now, that was possible. Or maybe God was dead too after what the Jew had seen.

God was dead and Trepov was Junger. And after Junger, what? It could be anything. The Jew shrugged and filed the incident away, a memory to be buried, but not forgotten.

By the time Junger reached his hut, his hands were shaking uncontrollably.

In the Camps, it was a habit to count time. He'd been there eight months three days, but from the moment he encountered the Jew from the carpet shop he began to fear for the future. For the first few days he was anxiously alert for any change, any hint of danger in the faces, the voices around him but then as time passed he concluded that the Jew had forgotten him. He even began to feel the thrill of playing with danger – he had, it seemed, been born with a lust for adventure, and an aptitude for deceit.

He was now, according to his new identity, a few months away from sixteen, still a child, and this afforded him some hope. A few months earlier President Truman had demanded on his own executive authority that the State Department set up consular facilities at the DP camps. He had added that special attention be devoted to orphaned children. This was a 'gesture' more than anything else. There were more than 250,000 Jewish refugees in camps, most of which were in Germany and Austria. The chances of America were remote.

The moment the 'consulate facilities' were set up Albrecht Junger went before the immigration inspector to apply for a visa and admission to the United States of America.

The immigration inspector barked a question.

'Why d'ya want to go to America, son? Why not England or France – Russia even?'

Junger shivered. He said: 'Because America is the land of the free, sir.'

The man smiled and said, almost under his breath, 'You better believe it, boy.'

'Sir?'

'Nothing. Look, they're free in France and England, aren't they? Why America?'

'No, sir. Not like America, sir. In America a man can be what he wants to be – under God, sir.' He had learned his lines well. Under God; the immigration inspector liked that. It was how he saw America. Everyone free, under God.

'I like you, boy.'

'Thank you, sir.'

'But not Russia, eh?' The great heathen, the anti-Christ, he thought. After they'd finished with the Nazis they should deal with Stalin.

'Not Russia, sir. Please, never send me to Russia. I hate the Communists.'

'Well, so do I, boy.'

Three months later he received the letter. His chest was constricted as, scarcely breathing, he opened the envelope. Then, sitting down on his bunk, he gave a smile of sudden sweetness mixed with not a little triumph.

He'd been awarded his visa. And 'Albrecht Junger' could be assigned to oblivion. Presently.

PART FIVE

THE CHASE

Chapter 1

David sat looking out of the window as the car moved slowly in the Tel Aviv traffic. The November sun was bright, but the season had turned and it was noticeably cooler than it had been a few weeks before. His body was relaxed, but his thoughts were busy. He wondered when he would next be back. You could never tell how long it would be before you were recalled for a debriefing. But he knew he must concentrate on more important things than geographical sentimentality.

Besides, he was now looking forward to the mission. The girl was not as unattractive as he had jokingly suggested to Avi. During the briefing, he had been handed a picture of a pretty blonde, laughing across a deckchair at a man who David recognised as his target.

'That's the girl,' Avi Lerner had told him. David had been sure of it. His interest quickened as he looked at the snapshot.

'She's attractive,' he commented. Lerner looked at him sharply, but said nothing and passed him the next picture.

They had not got far along the Haifa Road before they came to a jam with all four lanes blocked, traffic lights popping on and off as far as they could see.

'The traffic's appalling. I'll go the back way – we don't want to miss the plane.' Avi, who was driving, interrupted his thoughts.

'We've plenty of time,' David answered, but Avi was already turning sharp left into a side street.

'You're all set?' Avi seemed nervous, which was out of character, but then agents were often more nervous for each other than for themselves.

'Of course.' But still he went over everything in his head, mentally reviewing his brief.

They arrived at Lod airport, and Lerner handed David his suitcase from the boot of the car.

'Good luck' he said, and clasped David's hand briefly. They looked hard at each other for a moment and then Lerner was back in the car and driving away without a backward glance. David looked after the retreating car and then turned and walked into the airport building.

He checked in at the El Al desk and reserved a non-smoking seat at the front of the plane.

Four hours later, he arrived in Paris. He found a taxi easily and was driven to a small hotel in the Quinzième, off rue Bausset. He went straight to bed, but was up early the next morning, ready for his caller.

'*Monsier Avrim?*'

'*Oui.*'

'*Un Monsieur Bonnemaison est venu vous voir.*'

'*Très bien. Dites-lui de monter à ma chambre. Et deux cafés complets, s'il vous plaît.*'

'*Entendu.*'

David opened the door to a short smiling Frenchman, who was carrying a large Vuitton suitcase.

'You're in good time. I've ordered breakfast to be sent up.'

'Good.' Rule one. Never behave in the least bit out of the ordinary.

Until you pull out the gun.

They sat and talked in a desultory way until the waiter tapped at the door with the breakfast tray. He put it on a side table, pocketed his tip with a nod of thanks and withdrew.

The whole attitude of the men changed as soon as the door closed. The Frenchman put his suitcase on the bed and opened it. From it, he took out a fine linen suit and a Jermyn Street shirt. David looked amused.

'I know.' The Frenchman pre-empted any comment David might make. 'You've been to London recently; Jermyn Street is full of Continentals buying London labels. And the suit's Italian.' David laughed and went into the bathroom. A few minutes later he came back, dressed in the new clothes, right down to his underwear and socks. He handed back his own clothes, which Didier packed into David's suitcase.

'Now listen and think. Shoes, socks, pants, handkerchief, shirt, suit, tie, cuff-links?'

'OK.'

'Good. Now here in this suitcase is an entire new wardrobe, made to measure of course, which should cover every social occasion. Plus wash kit, razors, toothpaste, all that.'

'Not new?'

'Of course not. Here are your papers.' David picked up the perfectly forged documents and his new passport. 'David Lefèvre, born Toulouse, resident of Paris, occupation art dealer.' The necessary visas were stamped in.

'And Lefèvre?' The cover was usually a real person, either alive or in 'legend'.

'In Israel at the moment, taking an extended holiday. Photographs of your mother, who died two years ago, and your last girlfriend.'

'Marthe Auge.'

'Yes. Left you because you would not marry her – you don't see much of her any more. Now in this envelope are five thousand dollars, government approved for export. In the wallet, you'll find a Swiss cheque-book with the first few used, credit cards and business cards, and an open-end Concorde ticket to Washington DC. The art gallery does of course know about you.'

Alain Josef owned one of the oldest and most distinguished art houses in Paris. His family links with the Mossad went back to the Second World War when he had received not a little help from the Haganah (forerunner of the Mossad) in successfully removing several important works of art from Goering's bejewelled fingers. To this day he kept a bronze bust of Goering in his office, on which he would light the matches for his Davidoff cigars.

'He sends you his regards and hopes you do as well for the gallery as you did last time,' Bonnemaison said with a straight face, but a twinkle in his eye. David laughed. Last time had been eight years before, when as a cover he had set up an import-export firm in South America. He was officially buying primitive works of art, and had run the business so efficiently that he had made a handsome profit for his Paris associates.

'He's also set you up to meet some of his colleagues in Washington – this could be an instructive trip.'

'And, I hope, destructive,' David said to himself under his breath. 'OK, good, Anything else?' he asked aloud.

'Your watch.' David reached out his hand as Bonnemaison removed a long, flat, dark green box from his breast pocket. David opened the box and weighed the Rolex in his palm. He smiled wryly.

'I've never been given a gold one before.'

'Part of the image.'

David clipped the watch on to his wrist, and as he did so, there was a subtle change in him. It was indefinable, and he himself was hardly aware of it, but the Frenchman noticed it and knew it was time to leave. Bonnemaison

130

collected up the kit David had arrived with, and gulping down the now lukewarm coffee, shook hands and left.

David waited until he heard the heavy clunk of the lift doors and the groan as it started to descend. He then went into the bathroom again, and when he came out his new persona was finally complete. He had not wanted to offend Didier Bonnemaison, but there had been one missing element in the change of clothes. Any self-respecting Frenchman would smell deliciously expensive. David would now be spotted as a Frenchman from ten paces.

'CBS. Good morning.'

'Mark Schwartz please.'

'Putting you through.'

'Mark, Charles Langley here. There's something I'd like you to do for me.' Charles was using his private security cleared line from the Virginia headquarters of the CIA.

'Yes?' Schwartz's tone was guarded, but he knew the unspoken deal and was prepared to stand by it. He was a highly regarded political writer and his bi-weekly column from Capitol Hill was syndicated all over America and had a large following. Langley was his friend, and although the CIA man would never have compromised himself or his job by a hair's breadth, Mark was often the first to know of a press release that might interest him. In return Mark had occasionally performed small favours for the 'firm'. He never asked questions, and the two men were bound by trust alone.

'It's not too difficult. I believe you know Amethyst Barclay.'

'Brauner's girl? I've met her a few times.'

'That's good enough. There's a man I want her to meet. David Lefèvre. He's a Parisian art dealer, staying at the Ritz Carlton. I'm not sure how long he'll be there, so move fast. By the end of the week, latest. How's it sound?'

Schwartz thought quickly. 'I know she's become interested in buying art recently – not big stuff, but good. There's a gallery opening next week which I believe I can get Lefèvre invited to. Amethyst is a friend of the owners, so she should be there.'

'Great. Do your best to make *sure* she's there.'

'Fine. Give Lefèvre my name and we'll get together.'

Two days later David was sitting with a newspaper in the Jockey Club, waiting for his host. He had only been there a few minutes when he saw a paunchy middle-aged man dressed in a bizarre mixture of colours being shown across the room by a hostess. David could tell by the stranger's bearing that he was a man used to a certain amount of deference and yet as he drew closer David noticed a humorous glint in his dark eyes that detracted from any air of self-importance.

'Your guest is already here, Mr Schwartz,' he heard the hostess saying, and he stood up to shake hands.

'David Lefèvre.'

'Mark Schwartz. Pleased to meet you.' Schwartz wished he could find out a little more about this tall good looking stranger, but he knew better than to try and probe. Meanwhile, David was studying Schwartz and making his own mental calculations. He knew quite a bit about Schwartz, but there was still room for curiosity. He was sure Schwartz was a smart man, and not just at his profession. Their one conversation on the telephone had convinced him of that. Langley had told David of the total reliability of this journalist, and David trusted Langley enough to believe him. He just hoped that Schwartz did not have aspirations towards a whole new career.

The two men sat, David drinking Perrier and Schwartz a vodka martini, making conversation and summing each other up. Then as the waiter came to take their orders, Schwartz stopped his conversation dead. This was habit, however innocuous the subject. Washington thrived on gossip, and waiters were one of the best sources. Schwartz was obviously an old hand at the menu, and ordered quickly. David thought back to the days of his training when he was given a course in food and wine, and taught the difference between the eating habits of different nations. Now, as a Frenchman, he always put his glass down neatly in the middle of the place setting. No one would ever spot he was a fraud, but he, as a fraud, could spot another. Schwartz was bona fide.

David ate little and slowly, pacing himself to finish his first course of a salad at the same time as Mark came to the end of his Coquille St Jacques. The two men got on well after the first awkward preliminaries.

'Have you been to Washington before?'

'No. But I've often been to New York, and I've worked in Boston.' This was true. He had spent six months there on a duty assignment, but he had got 'hot' and he had been recalled to Tel Aviv to cool off.

'So you've seen some of our finest galleries,' Schwartz remarked with a trace of national pride, spearing the soft pink of a scallop fastidiously.

'I certainly have. Very admirable. You have some great collections. The Frick –'

'Not exactly true Americans,' Schwartz interrupted with a grin.

'Maybe not, but the Guggenheim –'

'Ah yes. And here?'

'Here I've only just started. I shall have to go back to the National Gallery at least once before I can even decide what I want to spend time on.'

133

'I must admit, I'm more likely to flash round in a hurry as a duty,' said Schwartz as he accepted his plate of roast beef and eyed David's sole. David did not believe him; he felt Schwartz had more than a grasp of art, and did not believe a fairy godmother had given him the knowledge at birth. 'And work? What exactly are you looking for?'

'I'm not really looking for anything specific, just to see what's happening on the market and perhaps go for some nineteenth-century American art. Wyeth or a Homer perhaps – the French like marine subjects.'

'How's the market in France at the moment?'

'Oh, not bad. There was a bit of a slump when Mitterand first came to power, but it's getting better.'

'I hear he's not very popular.'

'With our clientèle he's not. What amazes me is how no one expected him, or anything like him. We've had it coming for a long time. The upper classes were in a state of uproar for awhile. You'd have thought it was the Revolution all over again.'

'Have they started buying again?'

'Yes. Slowly. Anyway, we survive.'

'Of course.' Schwartz glanced at David across the table. His impeccable clothes, the soft gold cuff-links, the Lobb shoes and the general air of confident well-being did not speak too badly for the state of the French art market.

'Are you related to Archbishop Lefèvre at all?' Mark asked, and for one tiny fraction of a second David felt the adrenalin rise in his throat. Then he remembered having read about the Archbishop's refusal to give in to the Pope on the subject of Latin mass, and of his subsequent excommunication.

'After *Thorn Birds*, who knows?' he answered with a grin. 'I'm afraid I have never taken religion very seriously.' A half gamble, but at least he was telling the truth.

134

'If he still counts as an Archbishop,' Schwartz went on. 'I can never follow the ins and outs of Catholicism.'

David wondered what God he worshipped when nobody was looking. But he was not prepared to be drawn out on the subject of religion and the church, so after the coffee arrived he said, 'I have received an invitation to the opening of the Carolettis' gallery. I understand this is due to you? Thanks. I'm looking forward to it.'

'Oh, you'd have been invited anyway. I just made sure the gallery knew you were in town. Perhaps you'll find something to buy.'

'Will you be there?'

'Yeah, I might drop in – if I finish my copy in time. Tuesday's always my busy day.' They rose to their feet without any sign of a bill appearing.

Now that was true class, thought David. The world ran on odd lines.

David arrived at the gallery thirty minutes exactly after the time on the invitation. He had been told that Brauner and Amethyst were expected at a dinner party on the other side of town and didn't want to miss them. Nursing a glass of champagne David scanned the gallery. It was already crowded with the standard cast at such occasions. He was sure that it was the same crew that regularly showed up at Washington's soirées, gallery and restaurant openings. He hoped they wouldn't be too interested in a new face.

'David Lefèvre?' Turning round, David faced a silver-haired man in one of the best tailored suits in the room.

'Giacomo Caroletti,' he said, his hand outstretched in welcome. 'Good of you to join us.' While they were discussing whether the lighting could be improved on an Agam stained glass mural, a tall blonde walked in on the arm of a grey-haired, confident looking man. David

135

recognised the couple immediately, as did most of the people in the room. Heads turned and voices dropped as they were spotted. It seemed that a Henry Brauner entrance did not pass unnoticed.

'Handsome bastard,' David thought. He took in the cropped hair, the arrogant stance and aggressive jawline. 'Not a man to be tackled lightly.'

Amethyst accepted a glass of Bollinger from the waitress and turned, her eyes searching the room for her hosts. Seeing Caroletti she smiled, then appeared to do a double take as she saw the man standing beside him. Across the room their eyes met, and then smiling tentatively, half in recognition, she said a word to Brauner, who was already deep in conversation with a bejewelled socialite, and made her way across the room.

'Jack, how lovely to see you. I haven't had a chance to look around yet, but at first glance I'm impressed.'

'Thank you. And you're as beautiful as ever.' She was wearing a tailored off-white silk Ungaro suit and her skin was a soft brown from her Florida trip. She laughed and turned to David, a questioning look on her face.

'Amethyst, this is David Lefèvre, fresh over from Paris.' Caroletti introduced them, and giving Amethyst a quick hug, excused himself.

'I'm sorry, but I think we've met before, where I'm not sure – Paris perhaps?'

'I don't think so – and I'm sure I would remember you,' he added gallantly.

'How odd. You must look like someone I know.' There was still an air of doubt about her, but then she smiled warmly. 'Well, we've met now. I'm a fellow European. Are you here for long?'

'As long as it takes. I'm in the art business – over here to test the market.'

'So you must be knowledgeable on the subject. Would you show me around?' She gestured at the walls. 'I'd like to buy something – partly because I know Jack and Ann Caroletti, and partly because I'm interested in building up a small collection. Perhaps you could help me choose something?'

'It would be my pleasure,' he smiled. He was delighted at the turn of events. Not only was he taking the most attractive girl in the room around the exhibition (and he could spin that out satisfactorily), he was fulfilling his brief by doing so. Or was he? He felt oddly drawn to her. Perhaps it was *because* of the restrictions laid down by his Mossad superiors. He could hear Avi Lerner telling him, 'She is like the *Chanukah* candles. You can look, but not touch!' Did they have any idea what they were asking of him.

Leading Amethyst around the three rooms of the gallery was not a quick or an easy task. She seemed to know everybody.

'Oh, you'll soon realise that a few spins around the Washington social circuit and everyone becomes boringly familiar,' she told him. But looking into her dark blue eyes as she laughingly rejected an abstract muddle of reds and browns as a 'hideous jumble' he knew this was not entirely true. She could never be 'boringly familiar'. The painting in question was priced at five thousand dollars and was by a young artist who had received rave reviews on his first exhibition earlier in the year. Secretly David agreed with Amethyst but felt he should make the right art dealer noises.

'Abstract art is simply the interpretation of the way the artist sees or feels things.' Then, catching Amethyst's satirical expression he added with a laugh, 'It's always easier to read the title first.'

137

'I believe you're on my side after all. Be frank. It's nothing more than a designer label to hang on your walls. Is it?'

'No,' he admitted.

'And would you hang it in your sitting room?'

'I don't think I would hang it in my garden shed.' He grinned and they both burst out laughing.

Amethyst caught sight of Brauner signalling to her across the room, and looked hurriedly at the gold watch she always wore.

'Heavens, we must go,' she said as Henry wove his way towards her. 'We're going to be late. I've really enjoyed meeting you. It's much more fun looking at pictures with someone who knows what they're all about.'

'So come to the National Gallery with me tomorrow. I'll be waiting for you at the main entrance. Would twelve o'clock suit you?'

Amethyst thought quickly. Henry was leaving with the Senator for Iowa tomorrow for some sort of annual lunch, followed by a question time appearance at the Chamber of Commerce, and she had made no plans.

'Yes, I'd like that,' she said hurriedly, with one eye on the approaching Brauner. She said goodbye and turned quickly away.

For some reason she did not want the two men to meet.

The next morning, Amethyst overslept. For a moment she lay in bed, thinking over the evening before. She had enjoyed the dinner party – Geraldine O'Connor was becoming a fast friend – but it was to the gallery opening and the French art dealer that her thoughts really turned. Then she looked at the enamelled Cartier clock by the bed and immediately threw back the sheet and leapt up. Nine-thirty! Henry must have left hours ago. Shrugging on a robe, she slipped out of Henry's rooms and, making

138

sure that there were no staff around, crept barefoot to her own bedroom. The morning ritual always amused Henry. 'Must be a habit you English pick up at country house parties,' he would chuckle, but Amethyst felt she was doing the right thing; besides that, she liked to have all her own things in one place. She showered hurriedly and put on the barest minimum of makeup. The moment she was out of the bathroom, she heard a quiet rap on the bedroom door. It was Buster, perfectly turned out as always in black jacket and tie. Sometimes Amethyst wondered what he looked like out of uniform – whether he was a suit and tie or a sneakers and sweatshirt man. He was carrying a large silver tray with a pot of coffee, a china cup and a copy of the *Washington Post*.

'Mr Kelly says there's an article on the Senator and Mr Brauner that you might like to read. He's marked it for you,' he said, beaming and nodding towards the paper. He set the tray on a small table and vanished.

Now that the original antipathy between Amethyst and Kelly had faded, life was much easier for both of them. They hadn't fallen in love with each other, but each respected the place the other had in Brauner's life, and was careful not to infringe on the other's territory. In particular, Amethyst appreciated the long hours and real devotion that Kelly put into his work. This was a case in point. Before nine he would always have read the papers, and marked out anything that would be of interest to either Brauner or Amethyst. Kelly never worked less than a ten-hour day, and was often called upon to work even longer. He could not have had time for much of a private life – his whole existence was Brauner and the Republican party.

Amethyst poured herself a cup of coffee and picked up the *Post*. Mark Schwartz's column was neatly outlined in red.

139

Amethyst sighed. She didn't always agree with Henry's policies and had indeed had some tough arguments with him, over East-West politics in particular. But he always won her over – if only temporarily – by the sheer force of his personality and will. He always seemed so reasonable when he put his case.

'The only way to keep the world honest is to have an equal and opposite power,' he had stated one evening. She agreed. But thinking about it afterwards could find nothing equal to America's power.

Putting down the paper, Amethyst forced herself to break her train of thought and glanced at her watch. Already 10.30 – she would be late. She was looking forward to the morning's distraction. She had no deadlines to meet and for the moment had had an overdose of politics and politicians. It would be refreshing to be able to switch off completely and just have fun. Humming softly to herself, she looked out of the window to get some clue as to what to wear. It was a cloudy, overhung sort of day, and she chose a well washed pair of jeans, a navy Trussardi sweater and Maud Frizon pumps. Throwing a grey and blue tweed hacking jacket over her shoulders, she ran lightly down the stairs, carefree and invigorated. It was as if a part of her, dormant for years, was just returning to life.

When Amethyst saw David standing on the steps of the National Gallery she was unreasonably pleased to see him. She had forgotten how tall and how very attractive he was. David took her hand in greeting. For a split second, she was fixed by his pale blue-green eyes. Something in them made her pause – somehow they suggested something warm and familiar to her and she felt a goose walking over her grave.

'Are you cold? Let's go in.' He took her arm.

'Not at all.' She disengaged herself. 'I'm sorry I'm late. I got caught in the traffic.'

'I was afraid you weren't going to show up, and I've spent half the night reading the guide book so I could impress you with my knowledge,' he said with a laugh.

They moved slowly from room to room, walking through galleries filled with Rubens and Rembrandt, Dali and El Greco, until they came to the Picasso painting of 'The Lovers'.

'It was painted during the artist's neo-classical period,' David explained. 'Notice how effective his basic concept of involving the spectator is.'

'It's a very touching picture, isn't it?' Amethyst murmured, her voice a cross between awe and standard art-gallery whisper. She took a step back and suddenly winced. The spell of the painting was broken as, half laughing but with tears running down one side of her face, she said, 'It's not the picture – I've got a dart in my eye, or it feels like it. Sorry. It'll cry itself out in a minute.'

David reached out and pulled her towards him as with his other hand he took a handkerchief out of his breast pocket. 'Move over here in the light,' he said and gently tipped her head back. Very carefully he found the speck of dust in her eye and removed it. Then as he wiped the tears from her face their eyes met. And at that moment David fell in love.

He stood there, trying to keep control of himself. He felt breathless, stifled. He dared not move. All he wanted to do was pull that face, so alluringly, so temptingly near, towards his.

He felt Amethyst shiver. 'It's cold in here,' he said calmly. He was in control again. 'They keep the temperature at a cool fifty-five degrees – to protect the paintings. Let's get a drink in the café.'

Amethyst looked at him and smiled. He had wanted to

141

kiss her. She knew it – she had wanted him to. The thought made her happy, ill with longing and angry with herself.

They sat at a small table in the corner of the room overlooking the gardens. A waitress brought over a bottle of red wine and two chicken on rye sandwiches. The food and wine brought back their earlier mood of easy camaraderie. Amethyst asked David about Paris and what had made him decide on a career in the arts.

'I was brought up to it,' he answered dismissively. (Stick as close to truth as you can. Distortions rather than lies.) She explained her part in Brauner's professional life, telling him a syndicate was paying her for her 'on the spot' stories about the build-up to the Presidential campaign and laughingly explaining that she had two lives and had to be careful to remember what Henry had told her in confidence and what she could use.

'To do that successfully is a real talent,' said David admiringly, having precisely the same problem in his own career.

'Not at all – it's a knack and after a while you just pick it up,' she said, holding her glass out for more wine. 'Next I'm going to make my fortune writing a kind of racy, feminine version of *Making of the President* – you know, Theodore H. White's book.' David didn't know, but made a mental note to read it.

Soon the bottle was empty and David called for another one. They told each other stories, swapping bits of their past and laughing a lot. She spoke of her feeling of having met him before and ran through countless possibilities. Perhaps, she thought, taking in the white teeth and the arrogant curve of the mouth, he just fitted in with an ideal image lurking in the back of her mind. She had grown so fond of him so quickly that it made her uneasy. She glanced at her watch. Four hours had just vanished.

'I'd better be going.' Despite herself she felt disappointed that her day with David was at an end. He walked her to her car. She unlocked the door and paused. She wanted to say something, to let him know just how much she had enjoyed his company. 'I really enjoyed today,' she offered weakly. He smiled at her.

'I'm glad,' he said and then seemed to hesitate. She was in the car, engine running. 'Friday? Lunch at the Jockey Club? One o'clock? OK?'

'It's a deal,' she answered, pushing her hair back and laughing.

Only after she had gone did David realise how badly he had lost his centre of gravity.

Eastern 567 droned down the Florida coastline and from his window seat David could see the sunlight reflect dazzlingly off the dish of blue water below and then the flat brown stretch of the Everglades as the plane began its slow descent to Miami International. Florida had 1,350 miles of coastline, multitudes of privately registered boats and planes and a drug traffic with an income as big as the Federal budget. Money and power attract violence. It was the easiest place in the world to commit a murder and get away with it.

David's thoughts were broken into by the blink of the 'No Smoking' sign.

Amethyst surfaced once again. His mind kept slipping back to her, like walking on an icy slope. She and Brauner were probably already at the house in the Keys. David was a well calculated four hours behind them. He thought back to his last meeting with Amethyst two days ago. They had been walking slowly along the Potomac river above Georgetown and had stopped to rest at an old wooden bench.

'David Lefèvre, you are an unforeseen complication in my life,' she told him with a laugh. David liked Amethyst's laugh – it changed her face completely and made her somehow more accessible. Over the last few weeks since the day at the gallery he had discovered many things about her that he liked. The sight of her, and the clean, fresh smell of her took his breath away and made his heart uncomfortable in his chest.

'I didn't expect you in mine either,' he answered lightly.

'Then you'll be pleased to have some time off from me. I'm going to the Keys with Henry on Friday.'

The announcement had an odd effect on David. His brain clicked into top gear. Everything became brighter and sharper. He recognised the sensation and welcomed it as an old friend. His attention centred on Amethyst again.

'I was thinking of going away myself this weekend.' David smiled at her, but his eyes were blank and he seemed to be considering something.

'Oh? Where?' Amethyst had been surprised at her sudden wrench of jealousy.

'Nowhere special. I thought I'd hire a car and snoop around the state for a day or two.'

'Alone?'

'Alone.'

He had touched her hand briefly and she had withdrawn hers quickly. The mood between them was disturbed. She stood up.

'Do you know what, David? I think I shall miss you.'

She said it brightly, in the kind of voice the English reserve for making emotional confessions, and he had cautiously muttered something about his feelings being similar. There had been an uneasy silence until Amethyst took the initiative and picked up her handbag.

'I must go, David. I'm running late. Call me when you get back.'

'Of course,' he had said but she was already walking away with a clean easy stride, the swing of her hips wholly unconscious. She had left him without the customary kiss on the cheek. Somehow this oversight made the task ahead in Miami easier.

David was far from Amethyst's thoughts. She was standing at the foot of the bed in the guest cottage testing the weight of a dull metal object in her hand. She walked slowly towards the door. Henry was sitting on the sofa going through some papers in his briefcase.

'What's this?' she said tersely. He stood up and moved towards her slowly.

'As you can see, it's a gun.' Brauner was annoyed that she had found it. 'I always carry it.'

'Yours?'

'Yes.'

She turned the gun over. It was heavy and cold to the touch.

'Have you ever used it?'

'I've never had to. I keep it near me, just in case. Don't look so worried, it doesn't go off by itself.' Gently, he took the gun from her hands. 'Come outside. I'll show you how to use it.'

He rang Harold to warn him of the shots and taking a box of shells from a drawer, led Amethyst out of the house.

An hour later Harold saw them walking towards the main house and called to them in welcome.

'How did the lesson go?'

'She's got a killer instinct,' Henry answered. 'Once

145

she'd got over her fear of the gun, she was pretty damn good.'

Amethyst laughed. 'One-shot Barclay, that's me,' she drawled, cowboy fashion. But in the back of her mind the gun still scared the hell out of her.

David was off the plane and through the concourse sixteen minutes later. He had boarded the flight at Dulles with nothing but the clothes he wore and a small black canvas bag containing newspapers.

He went straight to the National car rental desk and using a Mastercharge card provided by Mossad in the name of Davidson, hired a Chrysler Reliant. His driver's licence showed him to be a resident of New York City. Mr Davidson of New York City then took the freeway, exited from the Coral Gables off-ramp, found a seedy, run-down shopping mall run mostly by Cubans, and used the Mastercharge card again to buy several floral-patterned shirts, some casual trousers, slip-on shoes, sunglasses, tanning lotion and other assorted accoutrements of a Florida holidaymaker.

He drove to a Sambo's, ate eggs but no bacon, and changed in the rest room. He found the freeway again, headed south, and then, at Homestead, once again left the freeway. There was one more purchase; at a camera shop he bought a Nikon F camera with a telephoto lens.

He rejoined the freeway for his journey south. Traffic passed him incessantly, ignoring the 50 mph limit, but David kept his patience. He did not wish to be stopped by the Florida Highway Patrol.

Two hours later, he was on the Keys, the necklace of islands threaded onto a man-made causeway stretching for one hundred miles and ending just forty miles from Castro's Cuba. David wondered if the people who sneered at the US paranoia over the Cuban dictator realised just how close Cuba was to mainland America.

He drove as far as mile marker 90, knowing that the house where Brauner would stay was just a couple of miles down on the West side of the Keys, close to marker 88.

It was to be there, at a moment of his choosing, that David would kill Brauner.

They had realised the possibilities of the place back in Tel Aviv when a plan had first evolved. The surveillance sheets had indicated that the Keys provided the best opportunity for the assassination. When Amethyst wasn't there, Brauner slept in the guest cottage alone; nobody would suspect anything until the following morning by which time David would be clear of the area. It would be carefully arranged to appear that one of the splinter groups of the PLO was responsible for the killing. It was plausible – Brauner's backing of Israel had already ensured his unpopularity with the Palestinians. The PLO would deny responsibility, but one of the extremist groups would doubtless take the credit. They always did.

But for now he turned the Chrysler off onto a rough sand and stone road, and rumbled down through palms and shrub to a one-storey, verandahed motel that looked like a relic from Bogart's Key Largo. A small pier jutted out into the clear water and beyond it boats of all shapes and sizes and all types were moored. There was the buzz of a power-sander and hiss of a paint-sprayer. He could see several men, one of them black, working on the boats. An incongruous neon sign proclaimed the place to be the Keys Motel, owned by the Tavernier chain.

David parked the Chrysler, took his camera and small bag, and went though the mosquito door beneath a sign saying 'Office'.

An old man who looked as if he had lived outdoors all of his life glanced up from a ledger. He had a stubbled chin and a growing paunch beneath his bibbed overalls.

'Hi. How'ya doin'?'

'OK. My name is Davidson, I have a reservation.'

'Sure you do. Took it myself.' He reached for a key. 'Cabin Eight. You here for the fishing? Maybe I kin rent you a boat?'

David held up the Nikon by its strap: 'Wildlife. Birds mainly, crabs, fish . . . you name it.'

'You'll still want a boat.'

David very much wanted a boat. 'Maybe that's a good idea.'

'I got all kinds.'

'What would I need? It'll be mostly inshore. I'm not much of a sailor,' he said with a laugh.

The man scratched his belly. David noticed his hands were brown and gnarled, a workman's hands or the hands of a fisherman.

'You git settled, git a good night's sleep, then come over to the yard in the mornin'. I'll get you sump'in' you'll like, sump'in' easy to flip around, flat draught, good outboard, s'all you'll need and I'll give you a special rate, you being at the hotel and all.'

'Water OK now?'

There'd been a bad hurricane in Florida just four weeks before.

'Sure, all settled down now. You'll git a bit of storm debris, few branches, trees and stuff . . . just keep an eye out and if it looks big, steer right around it.'

'Thanks. See you in the morning.'

The launch was fibreglass, short but sturdy, with two twin-plank seats, powered by an Evinrude outboard motor which also served as the tiller. The cost didn't really matter to David but the deal struck for the rent was generous, and David warmed to the old man.

148

He took his bag, his Nikon and telephoto lens, a couple of books on Florida birdlife he had purchased at the motel counter, and wearing only swimming trunks took the launch out about half a mile, then cruised the coast looking for Jay's house.

He recognised it immediately. The beach glared white in the sun; he could be looking at a film set of a desert island. He assembled his fishing rod, locked it into place, took out the Nikon and, attaching the telephoto lens, scanned the building and grounds. To anyone on the shore, David would look like a holiday fisherman taking the odd photo while waiting for a bite. Providence provided a flock of seabirds which settled in the water close by the beach. He twisted the lens into focus . . . and suddenly leaping into the image was Amethyst, in a brightly striped beach-robe, leaving the guest cottage.

He felt his heart pound. Amethyst! He followed her with the lens as she walked casually to the side of the blue pool. He watched her as she dropped the robe to the ground and then, as she dived effortlessly into the water, he tracked the lens back across the neatly-manicured lawn.

Then he saw Brauner coming out of the guest cottage. He was wearing a towelling beach-robe and carried books and papers under one arm.

David followed him with the lens like a sniper and wished passionately that he was holding, not a camera, but a high-powered rifle. Brauner settled in a sun-lounger and started to flick through some business papers. David presumed that was what they were, for every few seconds Brauner would make a mark with a pen he held. There was a movement of colour and David saw Amethyst come into view. She glistened wet from the pool and was laughing and shaking back her dripping hair, the water cascading in an arc as the hair whiplashed.

The first shot of jealousy hit him with all the jolt of a snakebite. As she walked past Brauner she kissed him lightly on the forehead. David could feel his temperature rise.

He lowered the camera. The jealousy had caught and was raging like a bushfire. He would get that bastard even if he had to die doing it. He tried futilely to suppress his anger. It is business, a mission, he told himself, as he realised with despair that it was not because of Brauner's treachery he wanted to blow him to bits, but because of his success with Amethyst. He sat wondering how, in such a short space of time, his professionalism had become clouded by emotion.

'The Mossad never kills in anger, only as an expedient.' David smiled grimly. You can take it, Avi, that when I kill Brauner I won't be angry, he said silently, in response to his instructor's voice echoing in his head. The girl means nothing. She has just proved a complication, that's all. But even now, as he sat in the boat mechanically adjusting the rod every now and again, he knew he was lying to himself.

He had never been in love before and was new to its rules and customs. He was not one for false sentiment and had treated women at their face value, which in the end is the last thing any of them want. But this time, for the first time, it was different. Perhaps jealousy was as much a symptom of love as the fast-beating heart; maybe all lovers felt as he did.

David stayed long enough to see Amethyst and Brauner stroll on to the terrace, where they were joined by a couple he presumed to be the Jays. He pressed the starter button on the outboard and whipped the boat around in a surge of wake. Opening the throttle fully, he raced off back up the coast. The engine vibrated, protesting against the punishment, but David kept the

Evinrude flat out until the boatyard came into view. He had, he reflected glumly, almost without noticing, caught three large fish.

David waited until Monday, when he knew Brauner would leave, and then he decided to make a landing at the house. He had made casual enquiries. Like the motel owner, most Floridians who had chosen to live on this precarious foothold in the ocean were open and friendly. They tended to respond to a casual enquiry with minutes of gossip. That suited David.

He learned that the house had a full-time housekeeper, plus an English butler and two groundsmen. There was something in the way his informant said 'groundsmen', with a mocking smile, that left David in no doubt that these men were guards.

David took the launch close into the shoreline until he reached the house, then waited, thirty long minutes. There was no sign of life whatsoever.

He nosed the launch up to what he recognised as a man-made inlet, the bank reinforced with now-rusting steel piling. He eased the launch in at minimum power. It was so quiet it worried him.

The inlet was over a hundred yards long, and curved, bringing the boats up to a picturesque jetty shaded by palms, in front of the house.

A voice said: 'That's far enough, mister.'

Instinctively, David killed the motor, and let the boat nudge the steel piling. He could still not see the owner of the voice.

'Hold it there.'

David held it.

He looked up.

A man had appeared, towering above him on the bank. The man was wearing a floral-patterned shirt not unlike the one David wore. The dark face was bearded. Someone had mentioned a groundsman called Cundo, a Cuban. David thought he had just made Cundo's acquaintance.

'This is private property,' said the Cuban.

'Pardon me?'

'You speak English, don't you?'

'Yes, I'm sorry . . . I mean, I didn't realise it was private property.'

'Didn't you see the sign?'

'Well . . . no . . . I . . .' David acted the part of the innocent tourist. Suddenly the Cuban's legs dangled over the side, and in an instant he landed feet first in the boat, rocking it dangerously.

'So why you here?'

'I'm taking pictures of birds.' David lifted the Nikon.

'Or maybe you're Press, hoping for a few candid shots?'

'What?' David feigned both ignorance and annoyance. 'I'm at the Keys Motel, ask them. I'm on vacation.'

The Cuban smiled dangerously. 'Maybe. Gimme the bag.'

David handed him the bag and the Cuban checked it.

David said: 'Someone told me you get flamingoes around here.'

The Cuban tossed the bag back. 'You get 'em in Miami Zoo as well.'

'I didn't mean any harm.'

'Sure you didn't.' The Cuban turned and hauled himself up onto the bank. The big automatic was clearly visible jutting from the rear waistband of the man's pants. The warning was obvious.

'Now turn your boat around and get the hell out.'

'Sure . . . sure . . .' David re-fired the motor, and gently turned the craft so it was facing to sea. 'I hope you won't report me for trespassing.'

The Cuban stayed silent. David remembered a sign he had once seen. 'Trespassers will not be prosecuted – they'll be dead.'

He headed out to the open sea. Clearly, the Cuban would be a problem.

Chapter 2

Amethyst flicked impatiently through the stack of phone messages on her desk. She was in the small ground-floor room which was exclusively her own for working and entertaining friends. There were message slips from her press syndicate, a fund-raising committee and even her old friend, Suzy Porter. But nothing from the one person she most wanted to hear from. Damn!

She dropped her handbag on the floor and flopped into the chair behind the desk. Why hadn't David called her? She knew he was back in Washington because that morning, on impulse, she had rung the hotel. They had informed her Mr Lefèvre had returned the previous evening. She had spent the following hours fighting the temptation to pick up the phone and call him. 'Must be going mad,' she muttered to herself and, reaching for a piece of paper, rolled it into the typewriter.

She had just returned from interviewing Geraldine O'Connor, the flame-haired temptress with the Jayne Mansfield frontage. The actress would add just the right amount of contrast to the other women in the feature she was writing on politicians' wives. Apart from Geraldine, she had done the interviews and research before going down to the Keys. She had been full of enthusiasm for the project, but on her return had found it difficult to concentrate on the job at all. The weekend in Florida had been fun and a welcome distraction, but it had given her space to think and she was surprised at the results.

She had thought of David. She had purposely tried to avoid it, but bits of him would flash into her mind at odd moments and distract her from the job in hand. She couldn't understand why this happened and hated the intrusions but seemed powerless to control them. Henry had noticed her sudden distractions and had gone out of his way to be attentive and loving, but he had not managed to dispel her moods. For the first time since meeting Henry, Amethyst had let herself admit that something was missing from her life. Now as she tipped back the chair and drummed her fingers on the desk top, she tried to define the missing element. She had everything a modern woman could ask for. A successful career that was important to her, a brilliant and powerful man with whom to share it, a pretty face, beautiful clothes, good friends.

She abandoned the list. She had been through it so often recently and knew that was not where the answer lay. One thing was missing from her life that had been there before David came along – peace of mind.

'You've muscled in,' she muttered. 'You've made me want all the things I thought I didn't need and dissatisfied me with what I've got. I'm not in love with you. It's a passing obsession. The seven-year itch – after eight months.'

She got up from the desk and crossed to the window. Irritably she tweaked the curtain straight. A corner of it came loose from the rod.

'Damn it,' she cursed, and rang for Buster.

'I've pulled the curtain down. Can you get Frank to fix it?' Her tone was unaccustomedly sharp and his smile faded. She noticed the slow fade and relaxed. 'I'm sorry, Buster, but the article's not going very well – I didn't mean to snap.'

The smile came right back onto his face. 'You sure

you're all right, Miss Amethyst?' he asked. 'Maybe's you comin' down with a bug.'

'No, I'm OK, Buster, really I am'. She was touched by his concern, and it eased her mood. Eased it but didn't break it.

Perhaps, in the end, all she wanted was a husband and children. She had adjusted up to this way of life and she could adjust right back down again. Henry didn't want any children. He had said so outright.

Somehow he made her feel old, whereas David brought back some spark that had been missing since – God knows when. It was uncanny but whenever she thought of David she was haunted by images of a family. She was nearly twenty-nine and if she wanted children, she had to do something about it very soon. Which brought her back to David again. She was obsessed with him – with the sound of his voice, with the touch of his hand, with where he was and what he was doing . . .

'*Stop it.*' She spoke out loud in an effort to stem her thoughts.

'Missy?' She jumped and turned. Buster was back in the doorway, this time with Frank, one of the groundsmen.

'I'm sorry. I was talking to myself again.' She gave a short, embarrassed laugh. 'If anyone needs me, Buster, I'm up in the music room.' There was no point in pretending to work. Perhaps Ray Charles would calm her down.

'*You promised me love, that would never die, that promise you gave was only a lie. You've found a new love . . .*'

She switched off the gramophone and shivered. What would she say to Henry? Her life was so caught up in his that it would be difficult to separate them and, besides, she still cared for him deeply. The sexual chemistry was wearing off, but that was partly her own fault – her growing obsession with David had meant that she had spent more and more nights in her own room.

Amethyst thought back to New York and the first time they had seen each other since London.

For once he had been early and she had opened the door to him wrapped only in a bath towel. In one swift motion he had swept her back into the tiny hall and yanked the towel away.

'So you missed me, did you?' he had said with his usual self-confidence. And pinning her to the wall, he had taken her there and then.

That evening she had thought that she was made for fidelity.

'Oh, why does life have to be so complicated? Why isn't it simple and direct instead of a series of conflicting desires? Doesn't anybody ever have it *all?*' she wondered.

'Ah, here you are.' It was Henry.

'Hallo, my darling.' Her guilt made her effusive. 'You're early. My article wasn't working so I came up here to relax.'

'Shouldn't you be getting ready? It's six o'clock. We ought to be leaving here in an hour or so.'

'Six o'clock, I must have lost track of the time.' She crossed the room and put her arms around Henry's shoulders, suddenly happy that he was there.

'Don't worry, I won't make you late,' she teased. Tonight was a big one. Party at the White House. 'What shall I wear?' Oddly enough, he always liked to be consulted on her wardrobe. He not only appreciated what she was wearing, but remembered and would ask after a dress if he had not seen it for a while. It amused and touched her.

'The new green one with the purple lights. You'll look a cracker in that.' She nodded – he had picked it out for her himself and tonight she wanted to please him.

As she sat at the dressing table her mind was firm again. She would say nothing to Henry. There was nothing to tell. She would say nothing to David – would not even try to get in touch with him. If he rang her, that was different. Anyway, perhaps it would all turn to nothing when she saw him again . . . If she saw him again.

From the moment the limousine swept through the North West Gate of the White House, Amethyst had the feeling that she had been spirited by a fairy godmother into an enchanted kingdom. She was no stranger to the political circuit but this was her first visit to the White House and she was determined to enjoy it. She had had enough of emotions the last few weeks, what she wanted now was champagne, laughter and a good long look at the President.

At the North entrance a Marine usher in full uniform greeted them. He glanced at the formal invitation.

'Good evening, Mr Brauner – Miss Barclay. Please.' He stepped smartly to one side, and Amethyst and Henry entered the Marble Cross Hall. Henry took her arm and led her under the immense crystal chandeliers to a bust of George Washington.

'Do you think he knew what he was doing, taking on you English?' said Henry with a twinkle in his eye.

'About as much as you do,' Amethyst replied, smiling, and glanced pointedly up at the red-carpeted stairs that led to the main Presidential quarters. They exchanged conspiratorial smiles as he led her through to the gold East Room.

She swept in on Henry's arm and felt a surge of pride for him. He was suntanned and fit and looked especially elegant in his dinner jacket. She felt good to be seen with him.

The room was already full of guests. All Washington was there, dressed to kill – made up and glittering. Amethyst caught the all-pervading whiff of power, money and opulence.

They spotted Geraldine, who was looking just the right side of tarty in a dusky-pink dress, cut low to show as much of that magnificent bosom as she could get away with.

'Hallo, darling.' Amethyst greeted her with a kiss.

'It's just like a scene from *Hello Dolly*, isn't it?' Geraldine bubbled. 'I've never been here before. You look stunning Amethyst, and I just love your hair up.'

Amethyst indeed looked stunning in the sea-green gown. Her hair was swept up and held in place by a thin strand of diamonds.

'Amethyst. Henry.' Sylvia's authoritative voice hailed them from behind. 'I thought you weren't coming. Been run down by a bus. You're late,' she said, all in one breath.

'Only a fraction. I know it's not on to arrive after the President.' Suddenly the room went quiet, the lights seemed brighter and the ceiling higher. The double doors at the far end of the room had swung open. The First Lady entered on the arm of the tall and undeniably handsome President of the United States. Heads turned and Amethyst felt briefly inclined to clap or curtsey.

The sound of the First Lady's high heels clicking across the floor accompanied by her husband's more measured tread was all that could be heard for a few seconds. Then the President greeted a guest and general talk broke out again.

Sylvia went on exactly where she had left off, her voice one of the first to rise out of the silence.

'They probably wouldn't have let you in anyway,' she said with a delighted whinny, and glancing about, lowered

160

her voice and smiled wickedly. 'By the way, did you hear that the First Lady fell down this morning . . . and broke her hairdo?' She gasped, then collapsed into uncontrollable laughter that was so infectious that everyone joined in.

Despite the grandeur of the room and company, the party went with a swing. Amethyst, high on the atmosphere and champagne, suddenly found herself face to face with the President.

'Mr President, may I introduce Amethyst Barclay to you?' Senator Ben Sharp was making the introduction. Henry's hand was reassuringly under her elbow. The President put out his hand. He looked surprisingly old and surprisingly kind, the blue eyes searching under the dark hair. She had the sudden feeling that despite his charm he was not a man she would choose to cross.

He was led away by an aide, leaving Amethyst impressed and thoughtful. She had recognised – within a fraction of a second – the monumental responsibility that Mother America was saddled with. She alone stood between God-given free will and the barbed-wire enclosures of communism. Amethyst felt a sudden distaste for European socialsim, in which envy was the ruling passion. She turned to Henry.

'I really liked him,' she murmured.

'Good. He seemed quite taken with you – and rightly so. Are you enjoying yourself?'

'Loving every minute.'

'There's Patrick. Come over and say hallo.' Patrick O'Brian was a political writer who tried, but had so far failed, to oust Schwartz from his number one slot.

'Henry, Amethyst. Good to see you.' Patrick broke off his conversation with the man standing next to him and gave Amethyst a wink. She did not respond. Secretly she thought him patronising and much preferred the rotund

Schwartz. Unabashed at her cool greeting, O'Brian introduced his companion.

'Have you met Carter Brown? Amethyst, I hear, has taken up an interest in art recently.' (Was this snide? Amethyst decided nót.)

'Carter is the director of the National Gallery.' Amethyst's heart jumped. Her mind flew back to her visit there with David.

'I was there only a few weeks ago.' She smiled and felt drawn to Brown, the only reason being that in some ridiculous way, he brought her closer to David. To hell with her resolutions, she would ring him tomorrow and damn the consequences.

'Amethyst?' The telephone had rung before she had got out of bed. It was David. She was awake instantly.

'Hi.'

'I'm sorry. Did I wake you?'

'No, the phone did. How was your trip? I was already beginning to think of you in the past tense.'

He laughed. 'The trip was fine. I got back late Monday night and spent the whole of yesterday tracking down a Homer that had come on the market.'

'Did you get it?'

'Sure, that's why I'm calling you.'

'You need my expert opinion?' She was laughing.

'You're impossible.'

'Only before my coffee.'

'How does tea sound?' David ventured.

'What?'

'Tea, English style. Cream cakes – the works.'

'When?'

'Tomorrow, my hotel.' There was a pause. 'Say yes.'

'Yes.' She was laughing and accepted without thinking further.

'Good. See you four o'clock tomorrow.'

For David, logically, it was an impossible situation. He knew that. Her feelings went against her loyalty to Brauner; his went against everything he believed in. For the first time in his life he was having to *remind* himself that his job and his duty came first. That he had to remain in touch with Amethyst to accomplish his purpose was one thing; to see her far more often than was necessary, or indeed wise, was another.

At the Keys, he had struggled hard to regain some control over himself and had been making progress – until the phone call, that is.

It was hopeless. As soon as he heard her voice, the rhythm of his heart beat and the eager tremble in his gut indicated to him just how deeply he felt about her. Why he had fallen so badly in love with her, or where it might lead, he had no idea. His mind swung between despair and hope, his soul alternately sick then soaring, as he turned the problems over and over again in his head.

To begin with, he was a fake. 'Amethyst, I love you. Oh and by the way, I'm not a Parisian art dealer. I'm David Avrim, agent of the Mossad. Spy and assassin.' Except he would never be able to tell her that either.

And then – 'Will you marry me? Oh, and by the way, that doesn't mean Paris, it means living on a moshav near Tel Aviv.'

Whatever he told her she would know that he had lied, lied about almost everything except the way he felt about her.

No, he could not allow himself the specificity of hope. As an Intelligence Officer, he had to lie and deceive to carry out a mission but, if he ever entered into the realm of fantasy and began to lie and deceive himself, only disaster could follow. He must resign himself to the facts. To do anything less would be in breach of the trust placed in him. Whatever, if events went according to plan, his next meeting with her could be his last. Suddenly the thought that after tomorrow he might never see Amethyst Barclay again left him mad with relief and wild with despair.

Amethyst, her heart lighter by several degrees at having spoken to David, hummed Edith Piaf to herself as she sat at her dressing table. David liked Piaf.

She was having lunch with Sylvia – they had arranged it the previous evening. Because of the company and the occasion they had been deprived of a good crusty gossip and meant to make up for it today. Tomorrow she would have plenty of time to draft the 'Washington Wives' article before meeting David for tea. What should she say to Henry? Well, he did not usually ask what she was up to. If he did have any doubts about what she did in her spare time, he never mentioned it.

Sylvia was not so reticent.

'Amethyst, honey, this has got to stop,' she shrilled over the chocolate mousse at lunch that day.

'What has?' asked Amethyst innocently, but she had an inkling, and dreaded the lecture she thought she was about to get.

Sylvia levelled her sharp eagle eyes on Amethyst. 'I'm not in my dotage yet, you know. Now what's going on between you and this Frenchman – this Layfever?'

'Lefèvre.'

'Exactly. You'll be getting a bad name. Has Henry said anything?'

'Of course not,' Amethyst said tiredly.

'Well, then, he's about the only person in Washington who hasn't.'

'Sylvia, you know as well as I do that Henry's away a lot these days. You go places with men.'

164

'Of course. But not always the same one. Why don't you take George with you when he's not with Henry?'

'Why should I go anywhere with George Kelly, who I do not particularly like, to cover up an affair I'm not having?'

Sylvia rallied like an old war horse to the sound of the trumpet.

'Because, Amethyst honey,' she said with a triumphant whinny, 'discretion is the better part of respectability and don't you forget it.'

Amethyst had not forgotten it and some of Sylvia's lecture had left its mark. But, she told herself the following afternoon as she swung through the glass lobby doors of the Ritz Carlton Hotel, she refused to be intimidated by the tattle-mongers. 'Tattle-mongers.' She repeated the word and smiled as if to reassure herself that that was all it was.

David was also having doubts about meeting Amethyst and it wasn't the tattle-mongers that worried him. it was the possibility of an intelligence agency getting a 'make' on him that was the cause of his concern. As he had weaved his way through the crowded room designated by the Ritz for tea, he had become aware of being followed by a pair of sharp grey eyes. They had belonged to an athletic looking man in his late fifties seated at one of the tables. Identification of foreign agents forms a major part of any intelligence organisation and the last thing David wanted at this stage of the operation was to be tagged by a Sov Bloc hood, or, for that matter, one of his CIA 'cousins'. With this in mind, he had chosen a small table at the far end of the room partly concealed by a bushy plant and had buried himself in a copy of the *Washington Post*.

'So here you are.' Amethyst's voice brought David to his feet. As soon as he saw her, chic and youthful in a cream sweater and grey slacks, his doubts about meeting her vanished. They exchanged greetings and she slid into the seat beside him.

'My, don't you look well. Where did you get that wonderful tan?'

David had thought this one out in advance. 'Under a sun-lamp,' he answered, smiling broadly. 'I've no need to ask where you got yours. How was Florida?'

'Fine.'

David thought quickly. This was as good an opportunity as any. 'Are you going down again tomorrow?'

'No, next weekend – I think. With Henry you can never be sure,' she added with a wry little smile.

She was right about that, David thought darkly.

'Now what about this tea you promised me?' Amethyst asked, adroitly changing the subject. She really didn't feel like talking to him about Henry. 'Cream cakes and all.'

'At your command, Madam.' Laughing, David signalled to a waiter and ordered tea and cakes for two.

'This is possibly the most English thing I've done since I came to America,' Amethyst remarked as she took in the very British elegance of the surroundings.

'What is?'

'Having tea at the Ritz, of course,' she replied, her eyes laughing into his.

He watched her for a long moment.

'Do you miss England?' he asked, thinking of Israel and of how often he had missed it. Until now, that is, when he could happily sit at this table with Amethyst forever and tell the world to go to hell.

'Sometimes.' Her voice was thoughtful. She would certainly miss David when he returned to France.

'When are you going back to Paris?' She felt compelled to ask the question but dreaded the answer.

166

David glanced at her. 'Not for a week or two.' The conversation was stalled by the waiter arriving with the tea.

'Shall I be mother?' said Amethyst, reaching for the teapot. David nodded and watched amused as she poured the tea with all the grace of a Japanese geisha. Then, after offering him a cake which he refused, she took for herself a chocolate eclair and fell on it with all the abandon of a schoolgirl. It was this odd amalgam of teenager and *femme du monde* that most fascinated David. Perhaps, he thought, watching her demolish yet another cream cake – perhaps she could learn to live on a moshav. But he forced himself to change his train of thought and turned his attention back to Amethyst.

'I feel like I'm playing hookey,' she giggled, putting down her napkin.

'You are,' he replied. And God knows, so was he.

'Would you like to see the painting? It's in my room.' Amethyst hesitated, Sylvia's lecture came back to her again, but with the wrong effect.

'Yes, I'd love to,' she said firmly. She was not going to change her behaviour for the sake of a few gossips.

As they got up to leave, David glanced quickly around the room. The man with the grey eyes was nowhere in sight.

There was an awkward silence as they walked down the long carpeted hall to David's room. He opened the door and fumbled for the light switch. They blinked as the light came on and looked at each other uncomfortably.

'I'll get the picture,' he offered. She nodded.

David went to his suitcase and unlocked it. Carefully, he took out the painting, which was wrapped up in a few shirts.

'How chic to travel with a Homer tucked up with your shirts,' she teased, as he propped the picture against a wall.

He turned to her, grinning. 'Well, what do you think?'

Amethyst studied the painting in silence, lost for a moment in a private past. A small boat struggled in dark stormy waters. The memory of her home town washed over her, she could *smell* the sea. A tiny figure on the deck could just be seen, fighting desperately, but clearly in vain. She swallowed back the tears. She was a child again, with the picture of her father's death never far from the back of her mind, obsessed with the image of his last battle.

David, watching her, noticed how deeply she was affected by the picture. He wondered what memories it had conjured up for her. It had had a similar effect on him the first time he saw it. In the wild romanticism of the seascape he had seen the brave spirit of the thousands of 'illegal' immigrants whose last hope was to run the British blockades in an attempt to reach the Promised Land. After the horrors of the world war, they had risked everything one last time for the chance of landing a small boat at the dead of night on the guarded beaches of Palestine.

Of course, she would not identify the picture with Israel's history, David told himself, turning away from her. Why should she? Once again he felt the misery of how far apart they really were.

'A drink?' he asked, opening the fridge door.

'What a good idea.' Amethyst turned to him smiling. 'Got any vodka?'

'Enough to kill a Cossack. Tonic?'

'No. Just ice.' Her eyes returned to the painting. 'Where did you get it?'

'I bought it from a private collection. A really eccentric old man who said it made him seasick. Thank God,' he said with a grin. David brought Amethyst her vodka and their fingertips met. He almost dropped the glass as an electric shock passed between them.

'Static electricity,' David said coolly. But Amethyst felt there was more to it than nylon carpets and warm dry air.

She said nothing and took her drink over to the far edge of the bed where she sat, legs curled up beneath her, just out of the direct light of the table lamp. David sank into the armchair furthest from the bed. Amethyst stared into her glass and thoughtfully stirred the ice with her finger. The action was so unsophisticated that it caught at David's heart. The deflection of light from the table lamp just reached her and in the soft glow he noticed the straight line of her nose and the ridge of her cheekbone.

Amethyst looked up and met his eyes. Their blue-green was more green than blue, the lashes surprisingly long, casting a shadow on his cheek. The tension was suddenly unbearable. Amethyst took a sip of her vodka but could barely swallow. There was something about the way he was looking at her that seemed to deprive her of oxygen. 'Go home,' something urged her. 'Go somewhere safe – secure.' Abruptly, she put down her glass and rose to leave.

'It's late – I must go,' she muttered, not really quite sure what she was saying. David rose silently, the blood hammering in his head, hating his weakness as much as he loathed her strength. In a daze, Amethyst reached the door and turned to look at him. As if through a mist, she saw his face drain of colour, heard his sharp sudden intake of breath. Something deep in her psyche cracked open and suddenly she was sure. As he took the first step towards her, she reached behind and turned out the light.

They met in the middle of the room. His eyes gleamed at her in the darkness, and his face was a pale glow as it bent towards her. As she felt his mouth on hers she closed her eyes and forgetting all thoughts of Henry, Sylvia and the future, gave herself up to love.

At eleven o'clock David was woken by the muted ringing of the telephone by his bed. He was immediately awake and, moaning softly, rolled over to turn on the lamp. The bed was still warm from Amethyst, her odour still among the rumpled sheets. He had certainly not solved any of his problems in the last twenty-four hours.

'Hallo.'

'David?'

'Yes.' Shit, he knew what was coming.

'Alain Josef here. How are things?'

'Great.' Why didn't he get on with it?

'Did you get the Homer?'

'Yes.'

'Good. I look forward to seeing it.' The art dealer sounded genuinely pleased and David was slightly mollified. But he knew what was coming next.

'There's a Turner coming up for sale in two days' time. I'd like you to check it out for us.'

'Of course. I'll be back tomorrow.' He hung up and immediately booked an early flight for Paris. He lay back on the pillows and did not bother to switch out the light. There was no question of his going back to sleep. Macbeth had murdered sleep. Only Macbeth had nothing to do with it. He was going back to Paris to be debriefed and one of the first rules was to hold nothing back. He knew he would tell the whole truth, and as sure as hell he was not looking forward to it. But, all things considered, he felt no shame, no shame at all.

★　★　★

When Amethyst slipped quietly into the darkened house, there was no sign of Henry. She gave a sigh of relief. He was probably still at the City Labour Council dinner.

She walked up the wide staircase, her hand as usual trailing up the bannisters behind her, but her mind was full of David. She went to her rooms and slowly undressed, finally crawling thankfully in between the clean linen sheets. What was she to do? Was she really to throw herself into a grand passion with a man who had mentioned nothing of the future? Was she ready to give up Henry and follow David to Paris along with his luggage? She loved David – but was it enough?

She heard Henry's footsteps in the hallway and holding her breath in a poor imitation of sleep, closed her eyes and lay still. The door to her room opened slightly and between her lashes she could see Henry's head peering at her in the dim light coming through the door.

'Goodnight, my angel,' she heard him whisper as he silently shut the door. Daddy always did that, she thought, as she finally drifted off into a fitful sleep. How easy life had been then. How easy until a month ago.

Just before nine the telephone rang. Amethyst woke, feeling she had not really slept, dim memories of her dreams chasing through her head.

'Yes?' she intoned sleepily.

'Amethyst. It's David.' She was awake now.

'I have to return to Paris. I'm at the airport. I'll be back in a few days.' He paused, but she said nothing. 'Amethyst?' His tone was urgent.

'Yes,' she said softly.

'I love you – very much.' There was another small pause. 'That's my tragedy.' She only just heard the words before he hung up.

She lay in bed and examined the cornice around the

171

ceiling minutely, blocking out everything but the pretty plasterwork. There was a knock at the door and Buster arrived with the coffee and papers. As Amethyst dressed she decided she was relieved at David's sudden departure. If nothing else, it gave her time to reach a decision.

It never once occurred to Amethyst that her fate, her love for David, was beyond her control.

Chapter 3

David presented himself at the immigration desk of Charles de Gaulle airport and handed the uniformed officer his passport. He felt no concern as the French official gave the familiar, dark blue booklet a cursory glance; for the simple reason that the French themselves had issued it.

After passing without difficulty through customs, he strolled over to the public telephones and digging into his pockets, came up with a handful of change. He picked out a *jeton* for the telephone, dropped it into the box and dialled a number. His call was answered immediately.

'*Oui?*' The voice was terse.

'Is Laron still interested in the painting?' David was correspondingly curt.

'Yes. He will be at the Café des Beaux Arts at two.' There was a click and David replaced the receiver. Two at the Café des Beaux Arts meant three at the Café Voltaire. Sometimes he enjoyed the evasions and cover-ups of his profession. Today they only depressed him. He looked at the Rolex – eleven-thirty. He had more than enough time for lunch and a stroll by the Seine. His movements as he crossed to the left-luggage lockers and locked up his case were automatic; his mind was blank as he buttoned up his overcoat and left the building to join the taxi queue. He looked up at the sky; it was heavy and yellow and the air was bitterly cold. As the Concorde had taxied in, the weather information from the flight deck had forecast

173

severe frost. It did not feel that far away. His depression deepened. For a moment he envied all the others, the ninety per cent who led normal, uncomplicated lives. Why the hell hadn't he decided to be a bank clerk in sunny Tel Aviv? As the taxi drew up at the Quai des Tuileries, he let out a short sardonic laugh. I'd probably have gone *meshuggener* he thought to himself, and after paying the driver he set off towards the Left Bank.

David took his time getting to his three o'clock assignation. He crossed the Seine twice to make certain that he lost any 'shoes' that might be following him. Ace agents know their assigned cities better than any policeman. They know all the entrances and exits of its major buildings and where most of its roads and alleys lead to. It takes a very clever 'box of shoes' indeed to keep track.

Satisfied he was clear, David entered the café dead on three and took a small table at the back of the room.

Most of the other tables were empty and only a few people sat at the bar. David had a clear view of the entrance and the street outside. He called for an absinthe and checked the time. Goldberg had three minutes to show. If contact was not made within that time, David could assume something had gone wrong – a tail, perhaps, that could not be shaken – and would then go on to the next pre-arranged spot in an hour's time. Two minutes had gone by and David was two-thirds of the way through his absinthe. He took another gulp at it and looked up to see Goldberg walking into the cafe.

'Sam! Only just in time.' He crossed the room towards him and the two men shook hands warmly. They were old friends and always pleased when business brought them together.

174

Goldberg and David sat down at the back table and ordered more drinks. They spoke in English as they always did outside Israel.

'I nearly missed you. Bloody traffic. I always forget how the rest of the world goes at half the speed just before Christmas.' David managed a smile, but Sam could see his friend was not on his usual form. 'What's up, David? Anything wrong?'

'No – just a touch of the blues.' Sam nodded and touched David's arm sympathetically. Coming out of deep cover often took agents that way.

'But nothing in particular?'

'No. I'm just not running on full throttle, that's all.' He fell silent as the waiter put two glasses down in front of them and sat watching as the melting ice turned the absinthe cloudy. 'Sometimes I just don't know who the hell I am, who I really am, under all the roles I've played over the years. And then every now and again I catch a glimpse of myself – and I don't think I like it.'

Sam chuckled appreciatively. 'I know,' he said. 'I used to get that too.' He drained his drink in one gulp and left a handful of coins on the table. 'Come on, let's move. I want to be ahead of the Friday night exodus from Paris.'

They drove to Neuilly in Sam's battered white Volkswagen Beetle. Its image did not fit in with David's smart appearance and Rolex watch, but Sam laughingly called himself a poor relation and the car shook with the effort of keeping to the speed Sam was determined on.

Sam's lighthearted banter on the journey succeeded in jolting David out of the depths of his gloom but as they drove through some iron gates in a solid brick wall, to Sam's cheerful announcement, 'Well, here we are – safe as houses,' his heart sank again. He wondered who was in charge of his debriefing. David glimpsed the shadow of a man against the wall, and then the gates clanged behind them.

The porch was lit and the house looked welcoming. As Sam and David slammed the car doors behind them the entrance door opened and a pretty blonde appeared in worn jeans and a bright green jersey. He smiled to see her. 'Hello, Maya.'

She kissed him fondly. 'Hello, handsome. The boss is expecting you. Upstairs, double doors on the right.' The house was an old villa, grand in a faded way. It smelt as though the windows had not been opened for months. David breathed in the musty smell as he ran up the stairs. What the hell was Dulitski doing here? he wondered. So it would be de-briefing at top level. He paused just for a moment before tapping on the door and stepping inside.

Dulitski rose to his feet as the door opened and he met David halfway across the room with a warm hug and an affectionate thump on the back.

'David, my boy, good to see you. Come and sit by the fire. The house is as cold as a witch's tit.'

David was far too restless to want to sit, but did as he was told and drew one of the faded chintz-covered armchairs nearer to the three-barred electric fire. The weak heat it gave off made no impression on the cold of the high-ceilinged room. Dulitski sat in the other chair and moved it nearer to the low table that separated them.

'America suits you. You're looking thinner,' he said, pouring whisky into two glasses. 'This should warm you. Sorry the glasses aren't crystal.' He winked and passed David a glass. David tried hard not to look into the huge gilt mirror on the wall behind Dulitski. A cobweb stretched dustily across it.

'The mirror cracked from side to side,' he muttered.

Dulitski seemed not to hear him.

'*Lachaim* – to life,' he smiled and raised his glass.

176

'*Lachaim*,' David echoed and smiled wearily back.

Dulitski reached for his briefcase and took out a small tape recorder. Before switching it on he looked at David questioningly.

'Feel fit enough to talk?'

'Of course. Let's get it over with, while my head's still in Washington.'

They talked for two hours, drinking slowly but steadily to keep the cold out. At the end of that time, the table was covered with notes and maps David had drawn. Dulitski seemed pleased but thoughtful.

'So how do you feel about it? Do you want your back covered?'

'Frankly, I think I can do it without a back-up team. There's no proper surveillance – they seem to be more worried about the odd intruder or thief than anything more serious. The Cuban guy is the only one who could pose any threat but once everyone's "housed" in their pits he shuts himself in the domestic quarters at the back of the house. On my own, I'll not be noticed at Tavanier and will be in and out in no time. And if there is a cock-up, there's only me to worry about.'

'OK. It's completely your decision. Apart from that you've raised no problem. We'll have no trouble getting the gun to you on your return and then the timing's up to you. Now, David.' There was a moment's pause as Dulitski studied his fingers and ordered his thoughts. 'Tell me some more about you and the pretty Miss Barclay.' David started involuntarily and looked intently at his boss.

'What?' He felt a nervous quiver in his cheek. He knew he had hesitated and then had answered too sharply. He hoped Dulitski had not noticed.

'No special reason.' Dulitski was smiling broadly. David suddenly felt intensely aware of every nuance in his speech and attitude. 'Just a natural curiosity about what you think of your half-sister.' The silence was like the inside of an airtight black box. David stared at his guardian in disbelief. The room closed in on him.

'My half-sister?' he stumbled over the words, and could hardly hear his own voice through the buzzing in his ears.

'Are you OK, David?' Dulitski's voice came from another continent as David forced himself to his feet and stumbled out of the room. He found the bathroom on the next floor and locked himself in. After throwing up violently, the buzzing began to recede. He filled the basin with cold water and dunked his head into it. As he raised his dripping face he met his gaze in the mirror above the basin and the first articulate thought came to his mind. 'Thank God. Thank God I didn't. Thank God.' The prayer reverberated around his head until he had to plunge it back into the freezing water. What heaven-sent strength of mind – and body – had stopped him he would never know, but he would never cease to be thankful for it.

He found a damp towel and sat on the edge of the bath, rubbing his hair and face. The cold drops ran down the back of his neck as he thought back to the night before.

She had reached behind her and turned out the light, and they had met in the middle of the room with a kiss that spoke of all their self-control and repression of the past weeks. It was two steps to the bed and without any conscious thought about it they had found themselves lying on it, in a tangled heap of desire. Her body beneath his was soft and supple. No words were needed to tell how willing they both were to make love. She had given herself to him entirely. She was his toy. But she was more than that. She was his love.

With a desperate groan, he had torn himself apart from her. He lay still for a moment, looking up into the darkness of the ceiling. She was silent, but then he felt her reaching out towards him and sitting up he turned on the bedside light.

Amethyst, her face bewildered in the sudden light, had asked what was wrong. 'Everything,' he had replied. 'Don't you understand? I love you. Not just with words or with lust, but with real commitment.' Amethyst had still not fully understood, but some of the pain had faded from her eyes. 'I don't want it to be like this – a hole-in-the-corner affair when we meet to go to an art gallery and snatch half an hour in bed. You're another man's lover, Amethyst. I want more than that.'

She had lain in his arms for a little while, and had then quietly got up from the bed, ordered herself, and with extreme dignity and a gentle kiss, had left him. To go to Brauner.

David's eyes were intent as he unlocked the door and went back down the stairs to Dulitski. Now that he had got over the initial horror he wanted to know more; the reasons and excuses.

He opened the double door slowly. Dulitski was in exactly the same place, surrounded by the papers and maps and staring into the weak red gleam of the electric fire. David watched him for a moment.

'You bastard,' he said at last.

Dulitski took the remark in his stride.

'I'm sorry,' he said. 'I rather hoped I would never have to tell you.'

David looked at him with contempt. 'Then why the fuck did you?' His gaze was met squarely. Dulitski had nothing to hide.

'I think you know better than I do.'

David's mind flashed back to the pair of grey eyes at the Ritz Carlton. Silent, he crossed the room and took up his place opposite Dulitski, but without looking straight at him. He poured himself another tot of whisky.

'How long have you known that – she – is my half-sister?' He could not bring himself to say her name.

'Since we started investigating Brauner. David . . .' Dulitski's voice hardened. He knew that the last thing David needed was sympathy. 'You have a choice. The facts or a bunch of flowers.'

David found the strength to smile wanly. 'I'll take the facts.'

'Good.' Dulitski followed David's example and took another drink.

'Why did you send me?' David burst out angrily. There was a short silence.

'Have you ever come across the theory that women often fall in love with men who resemble their fathers?' David's mind went back to their first meeting, to Amethyst's insistence that they had met somewhere before. No wonder she had thought she recognised him.

'I ought to beat your head in.'

'And I'd feel the same in your shoes.' There was another pause while David tried to rearrange his thoughts.

'When did my mother meet – Barclay?' There was no question of his using the word 'father'.

'Tangier.'

'Tangier?'

Dulitski's gaze returned to the fire and he sighed as his mind drifted back through the years.

'Your mother – Ruth – took the oath with the Haganah in 1938. You know that much already. By any standards she was beautiful – she had wide, very bright green eyes and the most amazing head of chestnut hair. She also had more than her fair share of charm and intelligence. Very few people could resist her. I was not one of the few.' He smiled ruefully, his eyes not shifting from the fire. 'She started cautiously at first. Under British Mandate no Jew could carry weapons – this law was very strictly enforced. We could be clapped in jail at a moment's notice for carrying so much as a penknife. But Arabs and women were almost never searched. So Ruth became one of our "carriers".

'Then in '42 she was chosen to be one of forty men and women to attend a secret course in Mikveh Israel, the agricultural settlement just outside Tel Aviv. By day they worked in the fields. By night they were trained as intelligence agents. Your talents come from your mother, David.' At last Dulitski looked at David, but he was silent, waiting to hear more. Dulitski sipped his whisky and continued.

'After passing out she was posted to the Mossad Aliyah Beth. That had been created by the Haganah to help carry out the so-called illegal immigration but by then it had broadened out to include espionage and arms procuration.' David nodded. This was Israel's history – he wanted to hear his mother's story.

'Early in '46 she was sent to Tangier. At that stage it was an international zone, administered by a Portuguese Admiral but run by an international committee of control which included (of course) the British. Tangier got rich during the war. It was a centre for smuggling, spying and whore-houses. With all those different nationalities living in such close quarters, secrets were for sale everywhere. I suppose Tangier was second only to Lisbon as a centre for espionage. During the last year of the war, and the years immediately afterwards, Tangier also became a centre for illegal immigration. For a European Jew with enough money, it was relatively easy to find a way across to Tangier. So that led to the next problem – a growing colony of Jewish immigrants queueing for passages to Palestine which was, of course, blockaded by the English.

181

'Of course they mattered to us, but Tangier was more important to us for another reason. It is opposite Gibraltar, and for the hundreds of British sailors – officers and men – stationed there, Tangier was the place to go for fun. The drink, the whores, the change of atmosphere – and it was only a short ferry-ride away. It was in Tangier that your mother became so important to us – and it was there that she met your father.'

Dulitski fell silent. David looked up questioningly. He seemed to have stopped altogether, but to David the story had only just begun.

Dulitski had put down his drink and was taking a thin file in a buff folder out of his briefcase. He passed it to David across the table. On the cover, neatly typed in Hebrew, were the words: 'Report of Ruth Avrim (deceased). Subject: Tangier.' It gave David an emotional jolt. In a detached way he was relieved that it had. For a while he had thought nothing would ever move him again.

'That is Ruth's own record of her activities in Tangier. Back then, it was a requirement of all agents returning from overseas duty.' David opened the file and took out a sheaf of papers covered in handwritten notes in English. 'Shall I leave you alone while you read it?' David nodded without looking at his patron. Dulitski stood up. 'I'll send you in some coffee,' he said and left the room.

David moved his chair closer to the light and began to read:

In May 1946 I was posted to Tangier at the direction of Eliahi Golomb, and joined our small (but very efficient) organisation over there. It was a vital transit point for receiving and rerouting arms supplies being blocked by the British patrols.

'I was sent with two objectives – first to mislead British

Naval Intelligence as much as possible; secondly, I was to investigate the background of a French widow, Marguerite, Comtesse d'Audurain (rumoured to be running an escape route for some important ex-Nazis.)

'The first task was relatively easy. My cover was Ruth Kowerski, the daughter of rich Polish landowners on my father's side and of a successful middle-class Jewish family on my maternal side. An easy enough cover to live up to, and close enough to the truth to get round any potentially dangerous questions. I found myself a job, ostensibly as a secretary for Daniel Cohen, who officially ran a rental agency. I built up many contacts– my line of work helped – and soon managed to confirm what headquarters had suspected. Not only was Tangier overrun with spies, but a significant proportion of them were double agents. The end of the war had put them in fear of redundancy. Any excuse to stay was good enough. So the job of planting false information was child's play. They lapped it up. The English were badly fooled again and again and meanwhile we were getting our arms supplies through in a steady stream.

'I was also building up social contacts – and even began to enjoy my life in Tangier. I enjoyed hotel life – as you know I am more at home with a gun than a frying pan. I was living in the Hotel Fuentes, in the Petit Socco area of the Medina. This area was carefully chosen, and successfully so, because it is such a busy, close-knit area that I soon became known by the locals. This offered me some measure of security.

'After a few months I secured an invitation from a Spanish friend of the Countess to a party on board her yacht – the Djellan. I made sure to meet and become friendly with the Countess, and Marga and I were soon fast friends – or as fast as we could hope to be with such a minimum of trust between us. I soon began to collect *facts about the background of this woman who was one of the most fascinating (as well as most dangerous) I have ever met.*

'She'd been involved in espionage since the end of the First World War. Her husband (now dead) was Pierre, Comte d'Audurain. Together they travelled the Middle East and she became known for her wit and beauty – and the pearls in which her husband traded. Marga then had an affair with a British intelligence officer, Colonel Sinclair. He was later found dead. She then divorced Audurain to marry a Wahabi sheik, Suleiman, and bought a hotel in the Syrian desert. With her new husband, she went, disguised as a man, to see the Ka'aba, the sacred black stone at Mecca. She is thought to be the only woman ever to have seen it. A real character, our Marga. However, she was caught and sentenced to death by stoning and was only saved by King Ibn Saud's personal intervention. She has friends in the right places.

'Meanwhile, Suleiman was poisoned and died, so Marguerite remarried her French Comte and returned to the desert hotel. A short while later the Comte was stabbed to death in the grounds of the hotel. Not a woman to take lightly.

'Still a great beauty, she took up travelling again, smuggling gold and trading in forged passports. She became involved with the Nazis and spied for them during the last war, after which she escaped to Tangier and arranged the smuggling of their top brass from Spain and the Middle East to South America. Adolf Eichmann, I learned, slipped through her network. Too late for us, God damn him. Like many of her "clients" he probably travelled on a refugee passport issued by the Vatican City.

'One discovery I made, which pleased me enormously, was that she was also involved with the Palestinian problem – it was from her I managed to get hold of that very

184

incriminating letter from King Abdullah of Trans-Jordan, photocopies of which I sent you from Tangier.

'It was at about this time that I met Gerald Barclay.'

David looked up as he heard a polite knock at the door. Maya came in with a pot of coffee and a plate of sandwiches and silently put the tray down on the table in front of him. She left without a word. David poured himself a cup of black coffee and, ignoring the sandwiches, turned back to the file.

'We met in the balcony restaurant at my hotel. Many British go there: the quality of the Moroccan food is good and the price right. I was sitting at the table behind him and as the waiter brought me my bowl of Harira he turned and asked what the soup was called. As he did so his chair collapsed beneath him (not the first time I had seen that happen – the chairs there are famously shaky) and one of my best catches literally fell into my arms. Of course we dined together. He introduced himself as Lt Gerald Barclay, stationed in Gibraltar. He had access to exactly the kind of information that would be most useful, namely the patrol routes of the British Navy. He was also very handsome in a clean-cut, old-fashioned English way, and had honest grey eyes and a zany streak which was totally unexpected and added charm to his good looks.

'It did not take long for us to fall in love. I began to feel guilty about extracting information from him and felt I could no longer function correctly as an agent.

'I last saw him six weeks ago, by which time I knew I was expecting his child. We walked up the hill to Kasbah and looked out to the Straits of Gibraltar where East meets West. In legend Africa and Europe were torn apart by Hercules. The rift in the mountain chain is still called the Pillars of Hercules. I had meant to tell Gerry of our child

but as I stood on that hill, I suddenly realised how far apart our lives really were, too far apart ever to be bridged. I kept silent about the child and as soon as I returned to Tangier I put in for transfer back to Palestine.

'This is the reason for my return. I am now three months pregnant and will have the child. It was conceived in love, and although I have turned my back on that love, I will not do so on its consequences. Love, as we Jews know, is too precious and too rare in this world to destroy.

'The Moroccans have an expression – El youm wa-er-rhodda – today and tomorrow. It is a philosophy that gives not the slightest recognition to yesterday. I shall now have to live by it.

Ruth Avrim. August 1947'

Suddenly David found himself crying, the papers loose on his knees, his face buried in his hands. This was not the agonising, tortured grief he had felt on hearing Amethyst was his sister. It was a deep, dull sadness. He was crying for them all – for himself, for his mother, even for Dulitski who could not win his mother's love. And for Amethyst, who had given him a glimpse into a world about to be closed to him again. Somewhere he must find his mother's courage and shut the door himself.

He heard footsteps at the door and looked up. It was Dulitski. He crossed the room and put his hand on David's shoulder.

'I told you she was a very special woman.'

David smiled through his tears. 'I guess you were right.'

'Get some sleep now. We can wrap things up in the morning.'

As David reached the door, Dulitski spoke again. 'You know what your mother told me when I tried to talk her into an abortion?' David shook his head without looking at his uncle. 'She said, "Aaron, spies have feelings too, you know".' David turned to look at Dulitski and what he saw in his uncle's face gave him more comfort than the wealth of understanding behind the words.

Chapter 4

It was raining heavily in Washington DC and David's overcoat was soaked through by the time he reached the yellow cab rank. He jumped into the first in line, gave an address and settled back into the worn seat. He barely glanced at the driver who, after a brief pause, nosed the cab out of Dulles airport and into the heavy downtown traffic.

David was deep in thought and consequently did not notice the driver's first amazed glance in the rear-view mirror, then the repeated glances and the widening stare of astonishment on the driver's face. For the driver it was a moment of sheer disbelief followed by elation. But once he had a chance to study his passenger, the elation settled into a cold hard joy at what Allah had delivered.

Had David's guard not been so fatally relaxed he might have spotted the plastic tag that proclaimed the driver's name to be Abdul Assiz. The smudge of colour on the photograph might have reminded him of a room in Paris, two frozen faces, a shot . . . an escape. Instead, David sat back in the cab seat and thought only of Brauner and the mission ahead of him.

There is an Arabic proverb: 'Have patience and the body of your enemy will pass by your door.' Abdul remembered it now. Here, only a few feet behind him, was his enemy; the assassin who had gunned down his brother in Paris. How could he forget that face or that moment that was frozen like marble in his mind's eye? A man framed in the doorway, gun held out. The shots, blood curling in an arc; Hamdi, his brother, slammed against the wall. Then the gun turning on him, Abdul: an instant, a fraction of time when he thought he also must die.

There was a squeal of brakes, and Abdul pulled hard at the wheel, narrowly missing another vehicle. Calm down, concentrate, he told himself. Don't give the bastard any cause for alarm. He looked again in the mirror. There was no doubt in his mind that his passenger was his brother's killer, no doubt at all.

The man had been after Machmud, their eldest brother who was a leader of El-Fatah, the terrorist arm of the PLO. But Hamdi, the scholar, the man of peace, had died instead. And the man who had pulled the trigger sat alive and breathing just a few feet behind him.

Abdul wished he had the strength to kill him with his bare hands, and shifting in his seat cursed Allah silently for his physical weakness. He did not choose to ask why Allah had delivered his enemy up in the back seat of a battered taxi.

After all, it was Allah's will. It had brought Abdul Assiz to America, first to New York, then Washington, seeking asylum from guns, feuds, history and revenge.

Now Allah had told him that he could not escape his history, his race or his destiny.

Abdul breathed deeper, trying to calm himself. He must be like the wolf now, he must be patient and stalk his prey. He had waited for what seemed a lifetime, he could wait a little longer.

Abdul pulled the taxi up outside the Ritz Carlton Hotel, and David pushed some dollar bills through the security slot, telling him to keep the change. Then he was out, dashing through the slanting rain, shouting for the doorman to collect his luggage.

190

After David had entered the glass doors of the hotel, Assiz pulled the cab out of the waiting line and switched off his engine and sign. He got out, helped the bell boy with David's luggage, then made a quick dash for the hotel, ignoring the doorman who was telling him that the forecourt wasn't a cabbie's rest.

He went through the swing doors cautiously, and saw David leave the reception area, a room key dangling from one hand. He hesitated and when David disappeared into the lift walked over to the reception desk.

'May I help you, sir?' the girl said, ice-cold, making it clear that 'sir' was a formality and the help only an illusion. Everything about Abdul, from his faded leather bomber jacket to his torn, worn sneakers, said that he didn't belong in the hotel.

'The fare, just got out of my cab – just picked up his key . . . he left something . . .' Abdul was deftly removing a silver ring from one of his fingers. He held it up.

'Yes?' the girl looked down at the register. 'That would be Mr Lefèvre from Paris.' She put her hand out. 'Leave it with me, I'll make sure he gets it.'

'Uhhu,' Assiz shook his head. 'Can't just hand it over, he'd have to prove it was his. You tell him it'll be in the Lost Property safe, National Cabs. Address is in the book.'

The girl eyed him with displeasure. 'Feel assured, you can trust me . . .'

'Sorry, lady, I don't trust nobody. First lesson I learned in America, don't trust nobody.'

Then he turned on his heel and left the lobby.

Mr Lefèvre . . . from Paris! *Paris!* He almost shouted it out. There was no mistake. It was him.

He ignored the irate doorman and got into his cab. He left the flag down and drove home to his cramped

191

one-room apartment in one of Washington's black neighbourhoods. He had found his brother's killer. Now there was only the matter of the revenge.

David ordered a club sandwich and switched on the television, turning the volume down to low. Taking a Michelob from the fridge, he sat on the edge of the bed, drinking the ice-cold beer straight from the bottle. He stared mindlessly at the television. Thank God they didn't put me in the same room as last week. I'm not sure I could have stood that.

The telephone rang. It was the reception desk. 'Yes?' He listened and said, 'No, it's not mine, but thank him anyway.' He hung up and went back to his thoughts and his beer.

He hadn't stopped loving Amethyst; his feelings for her were too deep for that. But over the last five days he had worked hard at channelling his love for her into a different direction. Sometimes it worked, more often than not it left him in despair. There was a rap on the door and a waiter entered with the club sandwich. David signed the chit and took the sandwich over to the window. Way up in the sky was a jet, trailing vapour. It reminded him of Israel and the moshav. He had often stood in the early evening watching the sky turn pink and feeling the air tremble as a Phantom or a Kfvir zoomed across it. Israel. His mother had sacrificed her private life for her nation. Now it was his turn to do the same. As he looked out across the darkening skyline he laughed wryly to himself. If he were to die on this mission he was in the right frame of mind for the occasion.

The telephone rang again. 'Damn.' He picked it up and pushed the half-eaten sandwich to one side. He listened for a moment, suddenly alert.

'Send it up, right away . . . Yes, please.' Replacing the

receiver he drank back the last warming dregs of the beer.

He hoped the parcel on its way to his room contained what he thought it did.

He double-locked the door after the bell boy had gone and put the parcel on the bed. It was unmarked except for his name, hotel and room number written in black felt-tip pen, and it was securely tied with heavy-duty Scotch tape and string. He noticed too the Mossad seal, a special knot and a cross-over mark of Scotch tape, a surefire way of telling that the parcel had not been opened and re-sealed. With the room-service knife from his tray he tore open the parcel, put the debris in the bin and the contents on the counterpane. It was a .38 Colt Python revolver, with a screw-on silencer. Beside it was a small, heavy box containing, David judged, about fifty rounds of ammunition.

He was glad it was a revolver. Automatics could jam; revolvers were almost foolproof. He stripped it expertly, laying the parts out on the bed. He could see that it had been recently cleaned and oiled, but he tested the barrel, using a handkerchief as a pull-through, and found it spotless.

He re-assembled the gun and dry-fired it, feeling the satisfying click as the hammer went home. The trigger had a nice light pull, not too heavy, but not so light that a shot could be fired by mistake.

He fitted and re-fitted the silencer several times, until he was satisfied with the snug fit. He brought the gun up and sighted it on the headboard. It felt right, nicely balanced. He felt pretty sure this weapon had been adapted so it was just right. He laid it on the bed carefully, making sure there was no fluff on the silk counterpane, then he broke open the ammunition box and checked each round individually. He loaded six and spun the chamber. Then he emptied the shells back into the box.

All the deception and the play-acting was over. It was time for action and he was glad. All his reservoir of emotion had been emptied in Paris, when Dulitski had told him about Amethyst. He was an agent again, a man prepared to kill for Israel. Dulitski had warned him, 'Don't try to be her knight in shining armour, David, she doesn't need that.' No, he would not do that. But what he *would* do was ensure that she was not around when Brauner died. He would not permit that, for personal reasons, but most of all, for the professional ones. He would call her tomorrow and find out if they were still going to the Keys tomorrow night. When he knew that, he would find some excuse, some diversion or reason to ensure that she was not at Brauner's side when the job was done.

Amethyst was on her second cup of coffee when the phone rang, the red light flashing on her private line. She checked her watch. Eight-thirty. She jumped a little – it might be David. The last time they had spoken was when he had called her from a payphone at the airport, one week ago precisely to the day. In the interim, she had promised herself that the next time he called she would tell him how impossible it was for her to see him again. He had to understand that she was happy with Henry, with her life, her job . . . Counting to ten, she lifted the receiver.

'Hello.'

'Amethyst? It's David.' She felt her resolve begin to melt a little at the sound of his voice.

'When did you get back?'

'Last night. What have you been up to?'

'Oh, nothing much. All work, no play,' she said, trying to sound offhand.

'Look, I must see you. This evening.'

Amethyst caught her breath. 'David, I can't, we're leaving for the Keys at three.'

So they *were* going, Good, David thought. But Amethyst must not be there.

'I've come back just to see you. We must talk, I've got to be back in Paris on Monday.'

'I – I can't, I'm sorry.' But she really wanted to say yes.

He could sense she was faltering and pressed home his advantage. 'You could catch a flight down tomorrow.'

Amethyst sighed. It was hopeless, she really wanted to see him. 'OK,' she laughed. 'You win.'

'Seven o'clock then, my hotel.'

She heard the click of his receiver and replaced hers, vaguely cross at her indecision but happy at the thought of seeing David again. What, though, would she tell Henry?

David went to his bathroom and sluiced cold water on his face. He was shaking from deceit, and from the sound of her voice.

She found Henry at the breakfast table, reading the *Wall Street Journal*. She kissed him and slid into her chair.

'Darling, that was Suzy,' she opened.

'What?' he muttered, eyes still on the paper.

'On the telephone. I'm going to have to follow you down to the Keys tomorrow. This afternoon is my only chance of seeing her.'

'What's the hurry?' Henry put down his paper, folding it carefully.

Amethyst found it hard to meet his gaze. She poured herself some coffee.

'She's just flown in and will be in a meeting all morning and she's only here till Monday lunch time. She is my oldest friend – I'd hate to miss her.' Amethyst felt herself turning red. Henry looked at her thoughtfully. Oh God –

195

perhaps he had heard of the rumours Sylvia had warned her about. Now there would be a scene.

But Henry surprised her. 'Well, that's OK, angel, of course you want to see her. I'll get George to change our take-off time; Harold won't mind. Have lunch with Suzy and spend the afternoon with her. We can leave at five. In fact, why don't you bring her down to Florida? Ring Mary and clear it.'

Amethyst nearly protested but suddenly pulled herself together. What did she think she was doing, jeopardising everything for the sake of a familiar stranger who had some kind of hold over her?

She buttered some toast to hide her thoughts and then looked up with a pretty smile.

'That's sweet of you, Henry, and sounds great, although I doubt Suzy will be able to come with us – she's meant to be working.'

'That's settled then. I'm having lunch with Ben Sharp at the Senate. I'll be back around four.' He kissed the top of her head as he passed her chair. 'Have fun.'

After Henry had left, Amethyst made several attempts to reach David. First his room number was engaged and then there was no reply.

'Shall I connect you to the front desk? They will know if he has left a message. Perhaps we can page him in the public rooms?' the telephonist suggested helpfully.

'No . . . Could you tell him Miss Barclay will not be able to meet him tonight?' she asked.

'Yes, ma'am. We'll be sure he gets the message.' As she hung up Amethyst felt a whole range of emotions stirring within her. She was sure she had done the right thing. And yet why did she wish with all her heart that she could have kept the appointment?

* * *

196

Abdul Assiz knew that his moment to fight had come. He sat in his room, a tin of stew simmering on the Primus stove that was his kitchen. His story was the story of the Palestinians in microcosm. He had known Palestine only as a myth, a place left behind. Some nights he dreamed of Jaffa and the old city, of the orange groves . . . But when he awoke it was to the realisation that Palestine belonged to the Zionists and he was an exile.

His Palestine was a transplant, a now permanent refugee camp, the original shelters of tents and shanties long buried under the extensions of breeze-block and adobe. It had schools and barbers, spice merchants and cafés, it was one of many spread all over the Middle East, an Arab bidonville containing an exile nation.

For the Arabs it was convenient to keep the Palestinians there in their squalor as a constant reminder of Israel's violent birth, and Abdul knew that many Palestinians hated their fellow Arabs, the Jordanians and the Syrians, Egyptians and Lebanese, with as much fervour as they did the Zionists. Hussein of Jordan attracted their special contempt. Trans-Jordan – Jordan – it was Palestine just as Israel was.

For Israel the camps were a constant reminder of why they must go on fighting for their existence. A reminder that here was a people who, at best, wanted them driven into the sea.

But for Abdul, and thousands of others like him, it had also been home.

He had grown up with tales of revenge, but he and Hamdi had not been warriors, they had neither the stomach nor the inclination for it. They had heard too much of blood and sacrifice, they knew what it meant when a suicide mission went to the borders of the Zionist state. It meant blood and corpses and the screaming, wheeling Phantoms swooping on the camps with their high explosives.

It was Machmud, the eldest, who had gone to the Fatah, Machmud who had run through the blazing fires, sprawled in the dirt with the Kalashnikovs of the instructors firing inches from his head. Abdul and Hamdi had believed in the power of words and of persuasion, of study and learning. They had believed that it was through study and respect that the Palestinian cause would best be furthered. They had studied in Amman, a brief spell in Moscow, then Paris, then suddenly all the words, books, degrees and studies in the world had come to nothing when an assassin's bullet cut down the scholar in mistake for the warrior.

So perhaps Machmud's way, Fatah's way, the way of violence, was the only way after all.

Abdul had come to the United States to study, to think, to forget. Even after what had happened in Paris, he had not had enough courage to dedicate himself to Al-Fatah and the terrorists. But he could not escape his destiny as a Palestinian. That was to be part of a death struggle from the day you were born to the day you died.

So Abdul knew his moment to fight had come.

He had fired à pistol – every Palestinian youth had – and a pistol would be all he would need. A pistol was small and easy to conceal, and at close range it was also deadly. Many of the taxi drivers carried one beneath the driver's seat for protection, so it would not be too hard to get one. He went to the payphone on the landing near his room and dialled a man he had drunk coffee with. Abdul told him a fare had tried to rob him that day, and where could he get hold of a gun, the so-called Saturday Night Special? The man gave him an address.

Abdul drove his cab to an old downtown hotel and climbed three flights of stairs, then knocked on a battered door. He was let in and a man reeking of booze opened a metal biscuit tin that was lying on the bed. He rummaged through the pistols and found a Special. It was snub-nosed and small. Abdul gave him fifty dollars, and another four for fifty rounds of ammunition.

He took it home, cleaned it, using 3-in-1 from the hardware store, loaded it, spun the chamber and then emptied it of bullets again. Then he crouched and aimed at the mirror. Click. Click. Bang. Bang. You're dead. As a kid they'd played Fatah and Zionists, the Middle East version of cowboys and Indians.

Now it was real.

The waiting paid off. Assiz saw David come out of the hotel and climb into the back of a yellow cab. He eased his own car out into the traffic behind David's taxi. It soon became clear David was heading for Dulles, and eventually Assiz saw him alight outside Domestic Departures.

Assiz parked his cab in a bay for resting cabbies, locked his vehicle and went into the airport terminal. It was crowded but he soon spotted David at a check-in queue for Miami at the Eastern counter. He watched as David handed over a ticket, checked a bag, took a boarding card and left the desk. He went over to an adjoining desk.

'May I help you, sir?'

'Yes. Can I buy a ticket for that flight? For Miami?'

The woman consulted the computer terminal. 'We still have coach seats, sir. Cash or charge?'

'Cash,' said Assiz, producing a wad of dollars.

'I should really sell you the ticket, then ask you to stand in line at the next desk,' said the girl, smiling. 'But I'll check you in myself.' She winked conspiratorially.

'Thank you,' said Assiz.

'All part of the Eastern service. Smoking or non-smoking?'

The Zionist didn't smoke, or hadn't in the cab.

'Smoking, please.' He did not want to sit near him in the plane cabin.

'Smoking it is. Just hand baggage?'

'Yes.' Suddenly, it hit Assiz. The gun! How would he get it through security? Perhaps as baggage it would not be checked. 'No, I'd like to check it, please.'

'You'll be quicker off at Miami, sir.'

'No. I said to check it.'

The girl's smile faded. 'As you wish, sir.'

'It's just that I hate carrying stuff, plus I want to buy some magazines, cookies, chocolates, stuff for the flight.'

She forced the Eastern smile back to her face. 'You *will* get a meal on the flight, sir. But there you are,' she handed him his boarding card and luggage chit, 'you're checked to Miami. Gate 17, boarding in about forty-five minutes.'

'Thank you.'

David read for most of the flight, totally unaware of the presence of Abdul, who sat sixteen rows behind him in the Smoking section of the Lockheed 1011. At Miami, David's bag was one of the first off the carousel and he went straight through to the Hertz desk. Assiz was out three minutes later, just in time to see David, with a yellow folder, walk out through the sliding doors of the terminal building. He was going to lose him. He saw a Hertz courtesy bus draw up and David get on, then the bus moved off.

Assiz thought quickly. It helped that he was dark. Miami was virtually a Cuban city, so he tried on an accent with the girl behind the Hertz desk.

'You help me, I meet a passenger from Washington, I supposed to meet eem here, by the Hertz desk . . .'

'Is he Number One Club?'

'What?'

'A priority passenger.'

'I don't know.'

'Well . . .' the girl consulted her list, 'I've got three off the Washington flight, Svenson, Moses, Jenkins . . .'

Allah, he was using another name. Moses? That was Jewish.

'Moses, that's the guy, tall dark . . .'

'Aw, I'm sorry, you just missed him.'

Assiz swore, actually in Arabic, but it was obvious the girl didn't know Arabic from Spanish.

'Look, if you take the courtesy bus . . .' She paused. 'No . . . it drops them at the cars, all they have to do is get in and drive away. The next bus isn't for about another,' she looked at her watch, 'four minutes. You've missed him, my friend.'

'I'll get fired now,' Assiz said miserably. 'I was supposed to stay with him. The guy, he doesn't know Miami. Say, which hotel was he heading for?'

The girl sifted through her forms. 'I shouldn't really be doing this . . .'

'Look, I get stuck in traffic, you want I lose my job?'

'Hold on there.'

'Back on welfare, that's all I need.'

'You're breaking my heart . . . Here it is. This is the contact address. He's going down to the Keys.' She gave him the name of the motel and the motel's telephone number. She grinned at him wryly. 'You've got a long drive, kiddo.'

Assiz didn't know what the hell the Keys were, or where they were.

'I guess so, but ees better than losing my job.'

'Yes, and if you don't want me to lose mine, don't tell him how you got the address.'

Assiz suddenly felt an irrational warmth for America, so free and open.

'I won't tell him nothing.'

He took the airport bus into town, looked in Yellow Pages and had called a dozen car rental firms from the bus station, before he could find one that would rent him a car without a major credit card as security.

With the aging, battered Pinto came a map, and he soon found what the Keys were, and where they were. He had 519 dollars and 47 cents left and a long drive ahead of him.

Assiz was a very happy man.

He found a room in the Fisherman's, a run-down motel, just half a mile from where David was. After a shower, Assiz drove the pale green Pinto into a picnic site, a few hundred yards from David's motel, that afforded a view of the small quay and boatyard. With a pair of binoculars borrowed from the reluctant desk clerk at his motel he kept watch.

An hour and a half later, he was rewarded with the sight of David walking along the jetty and climbing into a small boat. He watched him fire the outboard, and saw the small craft push out into the water.

Assiz locked his Pinto and walked to the quay. There he met a man in work overalls who hired him a similar boat, agreeing that Assiz could moor it off his own motel just up the coast, but demanding one hundred dollars as deposit. Assiz re-assessed his view of America. When you had a dark skin no one really trusted you.

He knew what he would do; wait in the lee of the shore, and when David made his next trip out to sea, Assiz would follow and kill him there, out on the water, dumping his body in the sea. He did not know what David was doing in Florida. Vacationing maybe? Presumably even assassins took time off. It did not really matter, it was the perfect place. Here he could kill the Zionist, leave his body to the sharks and be back in Washington before the man was even missed.

It might mean waiting all night. Perhaps the man was fishing; if so night was a favourite time for bottom fishing, popular around here, he had learned. But it would be worth every second.

He spent the next hour searching down the coast for a suitable place of concealment where he could also keep a watch on any craft leaving the jetty area near David's motel. Then he returned to his own motel, and bought a vacuum flask, filling it with strong coffee to keep him awake. He then loaded his gun and returned to his hideout. It was eight o'clock when he settled down to wait, watching the dusk settle, turning the water from turquoise to violet. His people had waited for almost forty years. What were a few hours against that patient vigil?

David made another reconnaissance, and decided he would go into action that night, while Amethyst was safely in Washington. There would be plenty of boats out. Hemingway – as David always thought of the old man at the motel – had told him that fishermen often went out at night, so no one would think it odd to hear an outboard motor.

The water off Jay's place was shallow. Hemingway told him it was chest height up to a quarter of a mile off shore, if you avoided the boat channels, so he could wade in unseen and unheard.

And kill Brauner.

David lay down and slept for an hour. Then he woke up alert and ready.

The coffee kept Assiz awake, but he had to pee over the

side of the boat three times to get rid of the excess liquid intake, and he was just buttoning his flies for the third time when he heard the distant bark of an outboard. He tried focusing the binoculars, but all he could see in the distant murk was a small boat, one man sitting in the stern. It could be David, but it might not be; it was impossible to tell at that distance. It didn't matter, he would have to follow. Anyway, most of the other boats he had seen that night had more than one man in them.

He started his outboard at the third pull, feeling the first sweat of panic in case the motor would fail him. Then he eased the boat out at its lowest speed, trying to keep the distant boat in sight.

David could see the glow-worm light from another small boat out fishing, and the distant sound of an outboard motor way off behind him. That pleased him; just as he had thought, a boat out at night would not alert the Cuban or any of the other security people at Jay's house.

He went on through the night, watching a pale moon begin to rise towards the Gulf coast.

At a point off the house, David killed the engine, let the boat slow, and dropped a heavy chained mudweight into the water. The boat began to turn in a lazy circle.

He wrapped the gun and silencer in oilskin, put on a pair of rubber swim pumps and slipped over the side with barely a sound. The limpid water reached up to his shoulders and David, holding his deadly parcel aloft, began the long, slow, careful walk to the shore.

Assiz heard the engine of the boat ahead splutter and die, and then killed his own.

It was difficult to see very clearly, but already a small moon was rising, and in the dim glow he could make out the man in the boat stripping off his clothes. Going for a swim? That was crazy. Surely? But the man was already over the side. Assiz lost sight of him for a moment and felt panic again. Then he saw the dark head moving through the water, something held above him.

The man was *walking* to the shore!

Why would the Zionist – for it must be him – why should he do this? Take out a boat at night, stop offshore, then walk to the beach, carrying . . .? Assiz held his breath. The man was an assassin. He was not on vacation at all, he was on another mission. The thing above his head would be a gun; someone in that house at the water's edge was another target of the Israeli war machine.

He re-started the engine, first pull this time, and eased it forward at crawling pace. This time the Zionist would be the victim, not the killer.

Amethyst had a headache, and she was the first to admit to herself that it was psychological. Brauner had been tetchy the whole day and there had been an argument brewing between them ever since they left Washington.

On the plane they had hardly spoken, likewise in the car on that now familiar drag to the Keys.

The atmosphere had hung there, and had built up in her head. She had declined dinner, staying alone in the dark bedroom, waiting for the pain to subside. Henry had joined the Jays in the main house.

She could hear the distant sound of voices. It was the low boom of Brauner talking to the Cuban guard, Cundo. She closed her eyes. She did not want a late-night argument. If Brauner wished to make up with her he could do it in the oldest of ways. They could couple silently, and let body speak to body. She heard the door into the living room of the guest cottage open, then shut, the clink of a glass, the splash of liquid, and she relaxed. He was having a nightcap.

She settled further into the bed. Then there was the all-too-familiar sound of rustling paper. He was going to work. That could mean hours. She had seen him work until dawn broke, snatch a few hours sleep, and still be fresh as a daisy. She debated whether or not to go in to him, to try and persuade him to come to bed, then instantly dismissed the idea.

Nothing could take the Brauners of the world from their work.

David saw Brauner and Cundo part, the big Cuban moving off to his quarters far away at the rear of the main house. Obviously, the man was satisfied there was no danger. David saw something move in the undergrowth near him, a quicksilver motion, registering in a micro-second. He tensed, then eased as he saw the lizard, pale white in the moonlight, dart again, remain motionless, then scurry nonchalantly up the side of a palm.

He sighed and eased his grip on the silenced gun, now held firmly but loosely in his right hand.

He moved stealthily towards the guest cottage.

Assiz came out of the trees, still dripping. He had come ashore a hundred yards further down from where David had trod dry land, and now he saw Lefèvre again, leaving cover, moving towards a small cottage from which a light burned.

Assiz raised his pistol, then lowered it again.

The man was too far away, and this pistol was notoriously inaccurate. It was a cheap, mass-produced killer, good only for a close target. It was a gun to be taken from drawers and used in anger, a gun for husbands to kill unfaithful wives, or wives to kill husbands. He would have to be up close, very close, the gun against the Zionist's head. Then there would be no mistake.

He would see the man's brains, grey and wet, just as he had seen the brains of his own brother.

Assiz walked on, following his prey.

David came to the edge of a window and peered in, carefully.

Brauner was sitting on a sofa, an attaché case at his side, papers on his lap and spread on the sofa beside him. There was a glass in his left hand.

The traitor. The most pernicious and deep-seated traitor since Philby, Burgess and Maclean. They had been traitors working their way to the top of a nation whose influence was on the wane. This man could have been at the right hand of the most powerful man in the world, the President of the United States.

Unless . . .

David kicked open the door.

'Brauner!'

A micro-second of hesitation. Paris. The man Assiz. Could this be the wrong man too? A mistake?

But Brauner's eyes told him. Wide and staring, and above all terrified. A man come to judgement.

David shot him once, twice, great, tearing silent blows that punched Brauner off the sofa, spilling him in a tumble of attaché case, whisky, splintering crystal and papers, down onto the thick, rich carpet.

David kneeled over his victim, put his silencer an inch from Brauner's head, looked at the hair, the skin.

And pulled the trigger again.

Amethyst sat bolt upright in bed. The crashing door, two strange popping sounds, then the noise of breaking glass and a heavy thud.

She grabbed at the bedside drawer. It took an

enormous effort to open it. She had no strength at all. The gun was there where she had left it, in case of . . . Someone was in the cottage. Why was there no sound from Brauner? The gun was in her hands now and she pulled back the hammer with both hands. The back of her neck felt icy cold, the walls of the cottage frail as rice paper. She fought back a wave of panic, and taking a deep breath crept unsteadily to the bedroom door.

Incredibly, Brauner's eyes were still open, his lids fluttering. David flinched. My God, how long did it take for the man to die?

He cocked the gun again, pressing the silenced barrel to Brauner's mouth.

He said, 'Traitor.'

'Assassin!' It was said in Arabic, harsh and guttural.

David wheeled, saw the gun, the face above it.

'Stay still, Zionist murderer.'

David was frozen, but his eyes flickered, trying to remember the man, place him, anything to gain an advantage. An Arab, clearly an Arab and the suggestion of something, a resemblance. My God! Paris!

'You killed my brother, Zionist pig.'

He's talking, David, talking, when he should be shooting. He's an amateur, take him now, David. Now!

A door opened. Both men turned; a girl with a gun. David faltered.

'Amethyst!'

She confronted a tableau. Brauner on the floor, blood, débris, two men with guns.

David! One of them was David.

David and Brauner, Brauner dead, shot . . . and this third man, this stranger with the gun . . .

The man had the gun pointing at David.

He was going to kill David as he had killed Brauner.

Then the gun was kicking in her hand like something alive. There were two flashes of flame and a stink of cordite.

Assiz hit the wall with a crack as the bullets slammed him backwards, fell forward with a surprised look on his face, then crumpled to the floor.

His leg twitched once, twice. Then he lay still.

Then Brauner gave a gurgle, a long sigh. There was a rattle from his throat and his head fell to one side.

She dropped the gun on the floor and stood rigid with shock.

He acted instantly. There were only moments, for Cundo would come from the house, alerted by the un-silenced shots. Crossing to Assiz, he prised the Saturday Night Special from the dead man's hand and put it to one side. Then he wiped his own gun carefully on a cushion cover and wrapped the warm fingers of Assiz around it.

Amethyst just stood there, deafened. She tried to form words but heard only a rasping sound inside her own head.

He went to her.

'Amethyst, listen carefully.' She looked at him, dazed. 'Listen. That man shot Brauner.' He pointed to the body of Assiz. 'I was never here.' David shook her mercilessly. '*He* shot Brauner. You *saw* him, then *you* shot him.'

He saw a flicker of comprehension in her eyes and loosened his grip.

'Amethyst . . . if you love me, if you love freedom, *I* was never here.' He pulled her close to him for one precious second and kissing her gently on the forehead, whispered something in her ear.

Then he picked up the Saturday Night Special from the carpet.

And he was gone.

Epilogue

The funeral was over. Henry Brauner, once Albrecht Junger, originally Alexander Trepov, Soviet agent, was buried with pomp and ceremony, mourned by the very nation against whom he had worked.

Dulitski and Charles Langley walked away from the graveyard and the biting Washington wind, and climbed into the back of the smoke-windowed limousine.

Charles said, 'Goodbye, spy. Ever think we should be in showbiz, not the spook business?'

Dulitski smiled, 'Who was it said, "Ah, but the game's the thing"?'

'Shakespeare probably. Hey, one thing you never did tell me . . .?'

'What?'

'How did you get the first break on Brauner?'

Dulitski smiled. 'Every Jew who arrives from the Eastern bloc is debriefed. Everything they can tell us, however minor, we glean from them.'

'Oh yeah, and some little Jewish refugee just *happened* to know that Brauner was a Soviet agent?'

Dulitski allowed himself a grin. 'Not exactly. One man told us a strange little story about his father. His father had known a young man called Alexander Trepov, played chess with him. The kid was brilliant, it seems. The immigrant's father knew of Trepov's father in Russia.'

'And?'

'The immigrant's father eventually found himself

in Treblinka. God knows how he survived. Then he found himself being shepherded west, away from the Russians, and ended up in an American DP camp. Then he saw the boy, Trepov.'

'This Trepov was in the camp. So?'

'So now his name was not Trepov – it was Albrecht Junger.'

'How could he be sure? Jesus, a whole continent on fire, everyone has a double.'

'Wait, Charles, don't be impatient, you drink too much coffee. Trepov had a missing fingertip. You see a lot of a person's hands when you play chess.'

'And Brauner too . . .'

'Yes.'

Charles shrugged. 'Three names, two missing fingertips, life throws up a lot of coincidences.'

'Yes, of course, but sometimes it is wise to check. For if this man Trepov *had* changed his name, and if he was in the United States . . . well . . .'

'So you checked?'

'We checked. First we followed Junger's trail from the DP camps to the United States, then his meteoric rise to fame as Henry Brauner. Even for the land of the free he was doing remarkably well.'

'You suspected Soviet money, a fat turkey in the States, a sleeper keeping him supplied, priming him, pushing him?'

'Yes.'

'Harold Jay?'

'Of course.'

'But you still had to know. Damnit, Dulitski, you had to know that Brauner and Junger and Trepov were the same. And even if he was a Russian, for Chrissake, we know how many poor Russian kids changed their names then. Who wouldn't, to get out of Stalin's Russia?'

'Not this Russian, for you see Alexander Trepov's father was a major in the NKVD.'

'Jesus.'

'We activated an agent, found the old man who was living in East Germany where he'd settled after the war.'

'And he confirmed the information?'

'Yes, in several ways. First the message came to us from the agent repeating that the old man thought Junger and Trepov were one and the same.'

'You said several ways.'

'Yes, the Vopos ran the old Jew down in a gutter.'

'Shit.'

Our agent disappeared into the Vopo barracks. We don't believe he will ever re-appear. And then we found that Brauner was Brauner at Ellis Island. Not before.'

There was silence in the back of the vast limousine.

Langley broke it by leaning on the soundproofed partition and rapping sharply to draw the attention of the chauffeur. He made a forward movement with his hand.

The limo sighed into life and purred off, down the cemetery road, between the white gravestones.

'Will the Intelligence Committee get to hear all this? In Jerusalem they'd rather they didn't.'

'They get to know what we choose to tell them.'

Dulitski nodded. 'Good.'

He leaned back in the gloom.

Thinking of Israel, of sunshine, of David and his half-sister, the girl Amethyst.

Of David's mother, of the early days, of his own youth.

Israel had been a dream, and now sometimes he thought it was a nightmare: inflation, racial strife, squabbles, internal politics.

But he loved it, God damn them all, he loved it.

It was a brilliantly sunny day and the fashionable

boutiques on Madison Avenue were alive with activity. Pretty women in linen suits strode brightly along the sidewalks and not for the first time Amethyst was glad that she had forsaken Washington for the vitamin-charged atmosphere of New York.

She ate the last of her salad and lit a cigarette as she watched the traffic hurtle by. She was waiting for Sylvia. Smoking was a new habit and one she must drop again now she was fully recovered. But meanwhile, she enjoyed the luxury of smoking in the open air and just sitting quietly admiring the activity around her.

Le Relais had been a regular luncheon spot for her meetings with Sylvia since the beginning of their friendship. And now, as an established resident of New York, Amethyst often popped in, especially when the weather was like this. With the plate-glass doors slid back, the restaurant had a sidewalk café feel about it.

Sylvia was, as usual, late, but just as Amethyst decided to signal to the waiter for coffee a limousine drew smoothly up to the kerb. The chauffeur opened the door and out stepped Sylvia, dressed like a peacock and twittering like a glossy starling.

'Amethyst, my lovely, what can I say?' She perched beside her friend with an apologetic smile. 'The traffic – you know how it is – José does his best, but –' she shrugged her narrow shoulders and then, studying Amethyst's face, interrupted herself abruptly. 'Darling, you look better every day. I do declare you look as lovely as the day I first saw you. Before – all that.' She gave a dismissive wave of the hand.

Amethyst smiled. 'And it's all thanks to you really,' she said warmly. 'If you hadn't picked me up from the carpet when I came out of hospital, I'd probably have been right back in there.'

'Nonsense. You're as strong as an ox and a survivor to

214

boot,' Sylvia said and caught the waiter's eye. 'Two expressos, please,' she ordered without consulting Amethyst.

In just such a fashion she had taken over Amethyst's life five months earlier. Amethyst had spent two weeks in hospital, the first few days under heavy sedation. The rest of the time she mostly cried. Sylvia had visited her every single day, fussing over her like mother-one-chick. Her affection and strong-minded commonsense had pulled Amethyst through the worst. .

Amethyst had had other visitors whilst in hospital. A tall fair-haired man with unflinching grey eyes had been the first on the scene. He had made it clear, in few words, that it was important that she fall in with the obvious version of events, and that the great American public needed no further explanation. 'Your co-operation is important to us,' he had said, patting her hand. And then more gently he added, 'And it will not be forgotten, Miss Barclay. We can be very useful to you in the future.'

He had passed Sylvia on his way out. She had demanded to know who was disturbing Amethyst, but Amethyst had not needed to ask; CIA had been stamped all over him. The following day she had made her statement to the county sheriff and the coroner. She had been word perfect. But only the words had been lies, everything else had been real – the sense of shock, of loss, and not a little outrage.

Amethyst had stayed two months with Sylvia and had never been back to Washington. When she rented her own apartment she had sent for the rest of her belongings. They had arrived with Buster, who was totally lost without Brauner. He had stayed, the only reminder of the past year.

'Amethyst, darling, you're daydreaming.' Sylvia had been prattling on without Amethyst really paying attention. Smiling, she sipped her coffee and tried to pick up the thread of the conversation.

'Last night was the best yet. I think you've really got into the swing of it – haven't you?'

'Well, the first few weeks were mayhem. Worse than my first day at the *Southsea Gazette*,' she laughed. 'TV news is a very different kind of journalism. Before, I always had time to ponder over an interview. On TV you just have to get in and go for it, and trust that your instincts are right.'

'Well, you certainly did that last night.' Amethyst was pleased at Sylvia's praise. She had a weekly slot with one of the major networks and last night had been her fourth show. She had been contracted a few months ago and sometimes the words 'We can be very useful to you in the future' came back to her.

'Have you seen Mary recently?' Sylvia changed the conversation with her characteristic abruptness.

'No. Apparently, she's gone to pieces!'

Harold and the Cuban had taken off in the jet within hours of Henry's death. The plane had disappeared over the Caribbean. The wreckage had been spotted and it only remained for the bodies to turn up, or for whatever was left to turn up. Amethyst strongly suspected that the only remains that would be found would be those of the unfortunate pilot.

'If you ask me, she's flipped completely. She's spending fortunes on recovery equipment to try and find Harold's body. I'd leave him in his watery grave, poor thing. It's perfectly dignified and rather romantic. He wasn't even that nice to her.'

'Sylvia!'

'Well, he wasn't. Now if I were her, I'd spend all his money on finding myself a nice new husband.'

'You're outrageous,' Amethyst laughed.

216

'Well, I can't argue with that. Oh my good Lord, I am running late. I'm off to get my nails wrapped. Have to have them re-done or I will look a sight. Now, I'll see you next week at your book launch. That will be exciting. I'll try to get Mary to break her widowhood and come too, representing a very wet Harold. Poor thing!' She kissed Amethyst's cheeks and picked up her bag. 'Oh, and darling,' she grinned cheekily, 'there's a simply wonderful man I want you to meet, just your type. Nothing to do with politics!' she added as an afterthought. Blowing one last kiss she disappeared into the limousine.

Amethyst watched the car move slowly down Madison Avenue and suddenly her heart gave a jump. She leaned forward, her eyes eagerly searching, but after only a second she leaned back disappointed. Why did so many men look like David? she wondered. And where was he? Who was he?

She had tired of trying to puzzle it out. Perhaps the key lay in David's last words to her. She had been deafened by the shots and stunned with shock, but she was still sure that as he kissed her, he had said, 'Goodbye, little sister.'

They played the game . . . with no holds
barred

Husbands
and
Lovers

the sensational new novel from

RUTH HARRIS

Four people living in the fast lane. Four people who
thought they had it all . . . and then began to have their
doubts.

There was Carlys, with a spectacular career ahead of her,
married to the handsome and successful Kirk. But he
wasn't enough for her . . .

So she turned to George, every woman's dream who had
other lovers besides Carlys; like Jade, the talented fashion
designer who'd been burned before but still couldn't help
falling for his charms.

So there they were: the Married Woman, the Single
Woman, the Husband, the Lover – lost in a tangle of
feelings and fantasies wondering if the real thing could
ever be found . . .

"A steamy, fast-paced tale . . . you'll be spellbound."
Cosmopolitan

0 7221 4862 3   **GENERAL FICTION**   **£2.95**

Sensuous, seductive, passionate and shocking . . .

 . . . charts the private traumas and public
scandals of studio boss Kit Ransome,
who stands to lose everything when
her picture, 'Last Chance', goes into
the most expensive overtime in the
movie business

Golden Triple Time . . . A dazzling tour de force of power and
passion set amid the glittering worlds
of movie-making and high finance,
where family secrets are laid brutally
bare, and destiny stands balanced on a
knife-edge

GENERAL FICTION   0 7221 3814 8   **£2.95**

A SELECTION OF BESTSELLERS
FROM SPHERE

FICTION

FOOTFALL	Niven & Pournelle	£3.95 ☐
PRIVATE AFFAIRS	Judith Michael	£4.95 ☐
STREET SONG	Emma Blair	£3.50 ☐
GOLDEN TRIPLE TIME	Zoe Garrison	£2.95 ☐
BEACHES	Iris Rainer Dart	£2.95 ☐

FILM & TV TIE-IN

MONA LISA	John Luther Novak	£2.50 ☐
BLOCKBUSTERS GOLD RUN		£1.95 ☐
9½ WEEKS	Elizabeth McNeil	£1.95 ☐
BOON	Anthony Masters	£2.50 ☐
AUF WIEDERSEHEN PET 2	Fred Taylor	£2.75 ☐

NON-FICTION

MY MOTHER'S KEEPER	B. D. Hyman	£3.50 ☐
BURTON: THE MAN BEHIND THE MYTH	Penny Junor	£2.95 ☐
THE DISAPPEARED	John Simpson & Jana Bennett	£4.95 ☐
THE LAST NAZI: THE LIFE AND TIMES OF JOSEPH MENGELE	Gerald Astor	£3.50 ☐
THE FALL OF SAIGON	David Butler	£3.95 ☐

All Sphere books are available at your local bookshop or newsagent, or can be ordered direct from the publisher. Just tick the titles you want and fill in the form below.

Name _____

Address _____

_____

Write to Sphere Books, Cash Sales Department, P.O. Box 11, Falmouth, Cornwall TR10 9EN.

Please enclose a cheque or postal order to the value of the cover price plus:

UK: 55p for the first book, 22p for the second book and 14p for each additional book ordered to a maximum charge of £1.75.

OVERSEAS: £1.00 for the first book plus 25p per copy for each additional book.

BFPO & EIRE: 55p for the first book, 22p for the second book plus 14p per copy for the next 7 books, thereafter 8p per book.

Sphere Books reserve the right to show new retail prices on covers which may differ from those previously advertised in the text or elsewhere, and to increase postal rates in accordance with the PO.